SOLDIERS DIE

AARON GRUNN

Also By Aaron Grunn

Alaskan Rivers of Blood

High School Freak

High School Freak 2

Cafe Assassin

Terror in New York

Alternative Book Press
2 Timber Lane
Suite 301
Marlboro, NJ 07746
www.alternativebookpress.com

2013 Paperback Edition
Copyright 2013 © Aaron Grunn
Cover Illustration by Nelson Lowhim
Book Design by Nelson Lowhim
Published in the United States of America by Alternative Book Press

Originally published in electronic form in the United States by Alternative Book Press.

Library of Congress Cataloging-in-Publication Data

Aaron, Grunn, [date]
Soldiers Die/ by Aaron, Grunn.—1st ed.
p. cm.
1. Thrillers (Fiction). I Title.
PN370-380.G786S65   2013
813'.6—dc23
2013944082

ISBN 978-1-940122-04-5
Printed in the United States of America
10 9 8 7 6 5 4 3 2 1

"A murder is three things: a reason, a kill, a discovery. If you're lucky, you get justice."—Anonymous.

Table of Contents:

THE DISCOVERY

Two men crept towards a house. A half moon and stars provided the only light. The men's eyes missed nothing and always maintained a glimpse of each other. When the lean one reached the front door, he glanced at his stouter friend, waited for a nod, and twisted the doorknob. They entered the house.

Their hearts were beating fast. Fear. But fear to these men was a primordial tool, one that kept them alert and aware of their surroundings. Each held a nine-millimeter handgun in one hand and a flashlight in the other. Their steeled arms revealed scars from previous engagements.

Inside, bodies lay everywhere. One by one, the men turned them over, shining lights in the their faces. After scouring the first floor they moved to the stairs, stepping over the beer cans, liquor bottles, needles, and cigarette butts.

"Dirty Euro trash," the lean one muttered.

The second floor opened up to a hallway with two doors on each side. They split up and moved into their respective rooms on opposing sides.

Empty.

With the same routine as before, they walked to the final doors.

This time the lean man's knob didn't turn. He gave his partner a cockeyed look.

The thick one nodded in acknowledgment and moved into his room. He heard his partner kick the door. Nothing. He turned to the hallway.

The lean man was standing in the open doorway. He stood still, not breathing. His weapon hung by his side. His eyes were locked onto something inside the room.

"What is it man?" the thick one asked as he walked next to his friend and followed his eyes to the other side of the room. The thick man flinched when he saw the girl's body. He took a few steps, hands reaching out to her body. As his fingers touched her chin, he fell to his knees.

The girl was strapped to a bed, a limb to each of the four posts. She'd been stripped naked. Sliced across her belly was the word *Voleur*.

The thick man let out an anguished roar. Tears rolled down his cheeks and ran over a deep scar on his face. Remnants of shrapnel from a simpler time in life.

The lean man walked over, placed his hand on his friend's shoulder, and squeezed. He said nothing.

As his partner cried, the lean man studied the room. A young man was lying on the floor next to the bed, fully clothed. His hands were tied behind his back, and his feet were bound together. His body had no marks except a clean bullet hole through the forehead. Blood, brain, and skull sketched a pattern on the wall behind him. The aroma of feces and blood made the lean man want to spit. The rest of the room was barren. A chill ran through his body. He was rarely moved by death, but that didn't mean it didn't bother him, especially when it was this ugly.

The lean man knew the French word on the girl's belly meant *Thief*. They'd now have to start questioning people. They'd use all the methods they knew. They'd find who did this. There was no choice now.

CHAPTER 2

"Is that her?"

"Yeah, I think so," Justin replied, squinting.

"Mm mm. Kinda hot, why didn't you tell me?" Sam made an obvious effort to lick his lips so Justin would notice.

"Fuck off asshole."

"I'm messing around bro. Jesus Christ, you're a sensitive man."

"Yeah I am, especially when it comes to my sister." Justin stopped when he could see his sister walking towards them. "It is her." Justin's face lit up.

"Justin!" Kate said. She ran to her brother.

"Kate!" They threw their arms around each other and hugged.

Sam stood beside them, staring at the reunited siblings. Justin had been talking about this moment for quite some time now. Justin and Kate had grown up together in a dysfunctional home where they couldn't rely on their parents, or lack thereof. As a big brother, he made certain she focused on her studies and didn't end up like so many of her friends; knocked up and with no way out of the town. After redeploying to Germany, he bought a ticket for her to come over and see him. Kate had a young face, but her body looked grown in. She was poised to break a few hearts, if she hadn't already. The hug ended, and Sam cleared his throat to get some attention his way. He knew it would be better to get introductions out of the way as soon as possible.

"Oh yeah Kate, this is my good friend Sam." Justin's nodded his head towards Sam.

"Hi, Kate, pleasure to meet you," Sam said.

"You too." Kate hardly gave him a glance.

The three of them walked over to the baggage carousal.

"What color is your bag?" Sam asked.

"Red, with a black X on it," she said and smiled when Sam gave her an odd look. "To make it easy to identify, silly."

"Real ingenious," muttered Sam. He turned his attention back to the luggage.

Kate went back to describing every single moment of her graduation. Her valedictorian speech had, apparently, been inspiring. Justin, enchanted by his little sister, bombarded her with questions.

Sam could only imagine how nuanced this conversation was going to get. He grabbed the red bag as it floated by. Without a word he walked away. They followed.

The night was spent in their hotel room, the siblings talking away. Their talk provided a background murmur that aided Sam's slumber.

Finally, the time came for Sam and Justin to return to their post and get back to work. The siblings couldn't help hugging each other good-bye.

Sam looked on as they gave each other a final hug and Kate jumped on her train.

"You're going to see her again soon right? So why the emotion?" Sam said. He'd always thought a dependent relationship was a weakness. Sam was rational and knew that being a lone wolf was not a feasible way to go through life, but he was able to dissect through any person, or feeling, to distance himself from anyone he wanted to. The only thing he truly appreciated was loyalty. This belief had grown strong throughout his life and was hardened in combat.

"Yeah, I know, but your ass wouldn't understand... It's just that. It's great to see her, you know?" Justin said as Kate disappeared into the train.

"Yeah, what ever. I mean I know it's cool and all, but..." Sam could see his friend was lost thinking about his sister. "So what now? She's gonna get boned by some greasy Euro trash guy?" Sam regretted the words when a crashing blow landed on his arm.

"You worthless orphan, don't talk about my sister like that."

"Calm down," Sam said, rubbing his arm. "Jesus, you know it's true, right? You know that's why chicks do these Euro trips. She's a woman with needs bro."

"I know, still..." Justin trailed off.

Sam glanced at his friend. "I'm messin' around Justin. She seems pretty grounded and smart."

"Yeah, she is, isn't she?"

"For her age, yeah, I'd say so."

"She deserves a good guy."

"A nice combat vet like me?" Sam grinned.

Justin shook his head. "No orphan is gonna date my sister."

"It's her choice man, and few can resist my fucking charms."

"Right, fucking prince charming himself. She said you were weird."

"What a cunt."

"Exactly, so leave her be."

The train ride to the post was spent in silence.

The next day was spent back in the barracks cleaning weapons and various buildings. Of course returning combat veterans meant would be allowed to either sleep or watch DVDs in their rooms.

CHAPTER 3

Their time to leave the Army came sooner than either expected. As decorated veterans they were getting a lot of respect. But both saw garrison life as bothersome at best. Here if someone merely kept their boots shined they would be promoted.

As time back in garrison went on, things returned to being dumber. Teams kept getting sent to do pointless details. Of which neither would have a part of.

One day, avoiding pointless work as they believed was their combat given right, they got a loud knock on their door. Justin's television had been especially loud, so he turned it down. But the knocking continued. Justin opened the door and there was his squad leader fuming. The squad leader, a Sergeant, outranked Justin and Sam, who were Corporal team leaders. But all this didn't matter to Sam or Justin, as this squad leader had spent the entire deployment in Germany. To them this was the ultimate insult, but the Army had its ways, and one was that rank mattered more than what a person did.

"What the hell do you two think you're doing?" said the squad leader as Justin and Sam walked into the hallway. "Do you think you're special?"

Sam and Justin glanced at each other, grinning from ear to ear.

"You think this is fucking funny?"

"Yeah, it is," replied Sam.

In the hallway their new Lieutenant was writing on a clipboard. Just as both hated their squad leader, they hated this officer. Unlike their last one, who had been through a deployment with them, this one had just come into the Army. He walked over to the scene.

"You two need to unfuck yourselves right now." The lieutenant pointed at both of them.

Sam couldn't remember the last time he heard a college kid talk to him like that, but he did remember Justin crushing the officer's skull with a right handed hook. The lieutenant flew a couple meters back and landed with a crack as his skull slammed on the tile floor. He attempted to get up but his head just slammed right back into the floor.

The squad leader moved to restrain Justin, but Sam took his action as a movement to hurt his friend so he hit him with a right hand of his own. The squad leader stumbled, but before he could recover Sam finished him off with another right handed hook.

"So what now huh?" asked Justin.

Sam looked at Justin, "I don't know." They had just been given their punishment for the incident. The Battalion Commander had remembered them and let them off with an article fifteen and a stipulation that they couldn't re-enlist.

Justin looked over at his friend, "no ideas huh?"

"Shit man, I figured on staying in, if it wasn't for that faggot LT."

"Yeah that faggot, we need to leave him a present when we leave." said Justin lighting up anther cigarette and offered one to Sam.

"Naw man," Sam waved his hands, "I'm trying to quit."

"No one likes a quitter Sam."

Sam huffed back a laugh and they sat in silence in their barren barracks room allowing the gravity of what had happened to soak in.

"Remember what you said about that waitress?" asked Sam.

"Yeah man," Justin paused as an evil grin crept his face, "I was only pointing out shit Sam, it wasn't meant to be a plan."

"Why not? I'm telling you right now that shit's feasible."

"You're fucking serious aren't you?"

"Of course I am, all we have to do is transplant everything we've learnt in Iraq to robbing these fucks."

"Okay doing it is not what I'm worried about, getting caught is what I'm worried about."

13

"Not an issue man, first we tell no one else, and I mean nobody, about this. No boasting, nothing"

"That goes without saying."

"Second we hit random spots and countries so there's no pattern to be followed, we don't stay at hotels where we're doing hits, so our names don't get associated with the crimes, and lastly we'll case joints only when we're sure we can't be ID'ed."

"You've been hatching this plan for a while eh?"

"It's all I can think of for now. We'll change it as it goes. Besides what else can we do? I know I can't handle going to a nine to five."

"There are other choices. Slightly more legal ones."

"Yeah I've already done that shit... I don't wanna be some degenerate fuck with a degenerate job, smoking pot, waving my fist against the man."

"What do you call this?"

"Taking a shit on his doorstep. You down?"

"Of course motherfucker, you know I'm always down."

It all went easily enough, a few hundred Euro here and there. They were getting pretty good at it but then it got boring. Or that's the excuse they used. Sam was troubled by the guilt associated with robbing random people for everything they had. At first it didn't bother him, the success it brought was addictive. Sam liked being good at something

A week later, Sam and Justin were walking down a pedestrian walkway in Granada, Spain, when a man came up to them. It was a beautiful day, an open blue sky slowly tinted as the sun set, and women everywhere wore fluttering dresses that somehow seemed to match the palm trees everywhere.

"Hashish?" the man asked and reached in his pocket expectedly.

"Naw man. We're good," said Sam.

They stopped on the side of the street.

"Why don't we case this guy and get his money? He has got to have a decent amount right?" Sam said.

Justin glanced at the man. "Sure." He looked back at Sam. "But it sounds pretty risky."

"So what? What's that pussy going to do?" said Sam.

They both looked at the dealer.

"Besides when we hit them, ain't no pigs going to come after us," Sam said.

They split up and tracked the dealer from a distance. After a few hours, he headed back to his place. Following, with one on a parallel street, they watched him walk into an apartment building.

They kept an eye on the door for an hour before they decided to go in. Justin picked the lock. They stepped inside while pulling on their ski masks. With their nine-millimeter handguns out, they tiptoed inside the dark and quiet apartment. They could hear the television and see its light emitting from what was the living room— the first room to the right.

There was a pronounced smell of weed. Peering into the room, they saw the dealer watching television and eating a snack. Slowly, they crept up to him.

With a look and a nod, Justin swooped forward while Sam remained behind, the barrel of his gun a mere inch from the dealer's head.

Beside the dealer was a bundle of money. When Sam reached for the stack of Euro's, the man blurted out a syllable, but Justin pistol-whipped him before any thing else got out.

The man collapsed, his eyes half open.

They grabbed the money and left.

Later in the car, they counted the money as they drove away from town, doing exactly the speed limit. It came out to more than double what they had made from all the previous hits.

They did a few more hits around southern Spain before heading north. They always made certain to keep their hits as random as possible, never getting too greedy.

It was never too hard. A couple times they met resistance, maybe a dealer tried to be a hero, or a few too many people were in the house. Usually a little pistol-whipping and some blood spurting did the trick. Sam's guilt soon dried up. He was more comfortable with this route in life.

CHAPTER 4

Sam and Justin returned to Southern Spain after doing numerous hits in France and Italy. No other place could mimic the vibrant life of this part of Europe. They walked around the town of Tarifa. This town, on the cusp of the Atlantic and the Mediterranean, was a windsurfing Mecca. The people of the town spoke of a history as tumultuous as the wind. Everywhere they went they could see Arab blood and European blood side by side. Arabic script was prevalent here as well. And the whole town smelled like palm trees, sun, and sea.

They strolled the streets looking for a dealer. It wasn't too long before they found one and, using the same method as before, they stalked then robbed the dealer. This time instead of asking for the places of where other low level dealers were, they asked him where his boss was.

The boss of this dealer lived in the same neighborhood, so they didn't have to walk far. But when they got to the apartment, they could hear a lot of noise coming from inside. They stood by nervously waiting for the noise to subdue. After a few hours a couple men left, and the noise subdued.

Sam was getting edgy. Every moment that passed by increased the chances that the dealer they'd tied up and knocked out would get discovered.

They decided to go in. They walked up to the door, put on their ski masks, and pulled out their weapons. The door was unlocked and slightly ajar.

They knocked.

Both had been standing with their backs turned to the door. Sam was looking through the slight opening and as soon as he saw a man get close to the door he nodded to Justin.

It was quick.

Justin donkey kicked the door twice in quick succession. The first hit the man's face, and the second sent him flying back. Justin grabbed the stunned man. Sam closed the door behind them and they walked in with their weapons raised. There was a short hallway and to the right was a kitchen with two more guys in it. Justin threw the still-stunned man with his two friends.

One was weighing some cocaine and another was counting money. All three were staring at Sam and Justin, frozen in shock. Sam and Justin each put their fingers to their lips.

Sam's heart pumped pure adrenaline through his blood. He breathed deeper just so that he could think a little clearer. In his mind, he always made an effort to keep both his eyes open, pay attention to his peripheral vision and maintain his front post on his targets. The essentials to close combat with a handgun. If no one got the jump on them, and he hit them with his first shot... Well that was a major leg up.

Sam saw one man reach in his pants. Out of pure instinct he pointed his front sight post at him and squeezed the trigger. The back of the man's head sprayed out. He went limp. Sam moved to the next man, who looked like he was moving for something as well, and pulled the trigger again. He heard Justin fire a shot.

All three shots went through their targets. All three were dead. One shot right through his nose, the second through his neck, and the third through his forehead. Sam and Justin looked at the bodies stunned at what had happened so quickly. It was always a little sickening to see splattered brains and blood oozing out of a just living person, accompanied with that fresh flesh-and-organs smell.

They found that two had knives. They looked at each other and shrugged.

"Stupid idiots," Sam said. A sudden movement like that had to be dealt with. In a situation like this it was best to err on the side of caution, caution for one's life. A saying they had been taught in the military still stuck with them: "It's better to be tried by twelve than carried by six."

Though the room was now a bloody mess, and they had three murders on their hands, they felt confident that once gone they wouldn't get caught. The police would look at rival gangs, not tourists. They still had to be on their way. One gunshot was been bad enough; three would certainly get the neighbors' attention. This wasn't South Central Los Angeles, after all. They grabbed the money on the table, stuffing their pockets.

Sam was hit with the feeling that he was being watched. He glanced up and saw a woman staring at him. Next to her was a young girl clutching a pink teddy bear. The glare off the bear's eyes muddled Sam's thoughts for a second.

When Sam stood up, the mother and daughter saw the rolled back eyes and the brains of one of the men spread across the floor.

Justin stepped towards the women. But the mother let out a scream. Justin's fists flew and knocked her unconscious.

Before the child could do the same, Sam walked up to her and wrapped his hand around her mouth. Then he shielded her from the view of what he realized was her father. "*Lo siento nina, lo siento*," he whispered into her ear. He took her back to her room and shut her door. They checked the rest of the house and left.

In the car they sped out of the city, trying to keep the speed as legal as possible.

"Fuck, man! How were we supposed to know a family would be there?" Sam said. He was furious. All he could think of was the look of horror on the girl's face. He wished he could have made her feel better. She didn't have to see that. And he'd left her alone in her room, her mother unconscious. "Did you have to knockout her mother man?"

"What the hell did you expect me to do? You fucking kidding right?" Justin said.

"My bad man, my bad." Sam knew he couldn't lash out at his friend for reacting the way he did. "I know you couldn't have done anything else, it's just a messed up situation, ya know?"

"Yeah that was pretty fucked up."

Up until this point they held the noble notion that they'd actually been doing some good, that they were helping clean up the scum of the world, and if they made some cash from doing those good deeds, well they made some cash.

Sam didn't care that they'd shot those three men. But he did care about the girl and what she saw. Why would anyone bring their kid along to see what all the gunfire was about?

They both sat in silence, not stopping until they were over the border. In the background the quick beats of jungle music played.

CHAPTER 5

Several days after Sam and Justin had shot the three men in Tarifa, they took a train to Amsterdam to see Kate.

Sam and Justin entered Kate's hotel and recognized the fecund smell of marijuana. The entire train ride was Justin talking up his little sister. Sam nodded politely and smiled, though inside he had wished for a train wreck to end the pain. Now Justin was getting a tirade ready.

Kate answered the door with half opened eyes and a cigarette in her mouth. Sam was shocked. She looked like she'd aged several years.

Justin and Sam walked into the room and stopped in their tracks. It looked as if someone had thrown a grenade in there. There were beer bottles and cigarettes everywhere. A heavy aroma of damp smoke hung everywhere. Sam's shock was interrupted by the sounds of Kate vomiting in the bathroom.

"Easy, bro," Sam said. He could see Justin steaming. "You know we've all done this kind of thing when we were younger."

Justin took a deep breath as Kate came out smelling like bile. "You eat yet?"

"I'm pretty hungry," replied Kate.

The three walked out, Sam walked behind them, smirking. At least the tension was accompanied by silence. This he could appreciate.

Justin couldn't believe his sister was doing this, just throwing her life away. There hadn't been a single moment spent together in which she was sober. When he first saw the state of the hotel room he was about to go ballistic, then Sam calmed him down. Later that night he met her boyfriend. He used every bit of his energy not to strangle the little bastard's neck. Justin had always been protective of Kate, not a single boy in their hometown was willing to ask her out, lest they felt his wrath. But this Damien kid was something else. She'd met him in Marseille; fell for his thick French accent and his dark drug dealing side. To Justin, he was just some skinny Euro trash, slimy and without a backbone.

Justin blamed himself. Back home he'd left town and rode with a biker gang for a few years. Riding, drinking, fighting. It was a tough life and one he was made for. Then he picked up an amphetamine habit. He was arrested and the judge gave him a choice of jail or the army. Even though he never told Kate about it, she must have known. Was this her way of getting back at him? He agonized over this for days. He regretted ever telling her to come to Europe to see him.

Their last night there, Sam walked into the hotel lobby as Justin was walking up the stairs.

"Hey Justin, where you comin' from?" Sam asked.

"No where. Just walking around getting my thoughts together." Justin paused, slightly dejected. You know..."

"Yeah, I know, but you gotta let her do her own thing man. She'll get over it. She's young. We've all done this. So know she's gotta go through her little experimentation phase."

"She's messing with some bad people Sam. I mean a little weed never killed anyone, but they're doing coke in there. And I don't even see her leave the room. I mean my little sister could very well become a crack whore. How can I just stand by and let this happen?"

Sam shrugged his shoulders. "I know man, it sucks but..." he said and paused trying to think of something better to say. "I don't know. Just don't lose it you know? She's a grown woman and she needs to make her own mistakes, or else she'll never learn."

"What about if the mistake is death, I'm supposed to allow that? I mean I can't expect you to understand man..."

For some reason those words stung Sam harder than he expected.

They walked up the stairs and to their room. Justin noticed his sister's room slightly ajar. He entered and saw his sister and Damien shooting up in the bathroom, one needle between them.

Everything that had been building up inside for the past few days, Justin released. He grabbed Damien from the sink and threw him in the bathtub. There wasn't much of a struggle. Justin was a lot bigger and had years of fighting under his belt. He held Damien down with one hand on his neck and with the other hand started to rain Damien's face with crushing blows. Justin's fists came down like boulders and within two punches blood squirted on the tile floor.

Kate, initially shocked by the violence from her brother, collected herself and tried to save the man she loved. She first looked to Sam for help, but he gave her a dull lizard stare, surveying the gore in front of him as if he were looking at a picture in an art museum. She screamed at him to do something, but he simply turned away. She moved to her brother and tried to pull him off, but he was much too big. She looked around for something to hit him with. She was certain Justin was going to kill her boyfriend. She screamed out at the others to help her, but no one came.

Sam noticed the other people in the room getting up. The noise of someone's face being bashed in is quite distinct. Even if you've never heard it before, you knew what it was.

"Get the fuck back, right now," bellowed Sam at the others in the room. He'd observed them on and off during the past few days, and even though they were drug dealers, they were low on the food chain and had neither the will nor the capacity for violence. One of them reached for a cell phone. Sam immediately kneed him in the belly. The intrepid hero fell to the ground with a gasping sound. The rest of them shrunk back. Just then Sam heard a crash and the tinkling of porcelain.

Kate hit her brother over the head with the toilet lid. She stunned him enough to throw him off her boyfriend. She immediately tried to pick up her boyfriend. "Baby, you ok?" She got a response she could barely discern. Damien was alive, but broken in several places. She turned to her brother who was getting up, still a little stunned.

"You asshole! Who do you think you are!?" She pushed him with all her might. "Look at what you did!" She pointed to her boyfriend.

"What do you mean? I was helping you out." Justin paused as he rubbed the blood on his head. "He's going to get you killed."

"I can do whatever I want, with whoever I want!"

"Who cares about him?" Justin nodded towards her boyfriend. "He's a shit-bag. I can't believe you don't see that."

"Screw you. I love him. I'm not a little girl anymore. And I'll screw whoever I want." She could feel her blood boiling. She never wanted to see her brother again.

"Look Kate, I'm looking out for you, he doesn't care about you."

"How do you know that? I don't need you to look out for me anymore."

Sam edged over. "We'd better go, Justin."

Justin brushed him off. "You need to get away from this guy, Kate."

"Screw you, I hate you, just leave," she said and pushed him again. Justin hardly budged, but his face seemed to soften.

Some sirens blared in the distance. Sam grabbed Justin with both hands. "Justin, we gotta go now!" He yanked with all his might, and Justin finally relented.

"I don't ever want to see you again!" Kate gave one more blast from her lungs then fell to the ground sobbing. Her boyfriend was barely recognizable. She held his head and with a towel started to soak the blood off his face.

CHAPTER 6

At Sam's insistence they left Amsterdam. Sam was afraid the police there would be looking for them. He was probably right. But there was still the matter of Kate.

Justin had never felt so alone before in his life. He had always been there for his sister. More importantly her presence had always calmed him down, clarified his thoughts. With her he knew there was someone else there with him.

There were still a chance that he could see her again. Most likely she left Amsterdam. Justin knew Damien had a home in Marseille, where Damien's parents lived. He would have to go there sooner or later. There was no other choice.

They didn't go immediately. Sam, paranoid as always, decided to stop in Paris for a few days. He had a friend they could stay with. And it took more than a week before Sam was fully satisfied that the situation was clear and agreed to move on to Marseille.

As soon as they arrived in Marseille they started to look around. One day walking down a street, Sam recognized the man who was in Kate's entourage in Amsterdam—the one who tried to be a hero. They followed, only a few meters behind. The man turned the corner into an alley.

"*Pardon!*" Sam yelled out, putting on his best French accent. No sooner did the words leave his mouth did the two of them start sprinting towards the man.

Maxime turned his head with a curious look on his face. "*Oui?*" He turned around. Before he could back up or defend himself, the bigger one grabbed his arm and muscled him to the wall. He covered his face with one hand when he saw a cocked fist. He turned away and when no punch came, he turned back. The lean one was holding the hand back. Then he recognized the faces: the crazy American from Amsterdam and his quiet friend.

"Where's his sister?" The quiet one hissed.

"I don't know what you're talking about man, I've got no money," said Maxime.

"Oh great." The quiet one rolled his eyes and pulled out a knife. "I know you remember us, you were the asshole who tried to call the cops on us." He nodded at his big crazy friend who twisted the kid's arm and brought him to the ground. "We're not fuckin' around kid. Tell us, or there is going to be some fucking pain." He pushed the knife under Maxime's eyeball. "Don't move. You'll hurt yourself."

Maxime saw something in the quiet one's eyes that he had seen in that hotel room in Amsterdam. Coldness. It enveloped those eyes. Any chance at pity was gone. Maxime remembered those eyes as they'd looked on impassively as his friend was brutally beaten. "Okay, okay," Maxime said and raised his hands. "I don't know, but I think they're about to leave the city."

"Give me an address."

"All right, just put that knife away." Maxime wanted to be done with these two psychopaths.

"You don't get any fucking room for any fucking requests asshole," Sam hissed between his gritted teeth and pushed the knife even harder against Maxime's eyeball.

Maxime could feel his eyeball shriek with pain, and his vision turn white. He decided to rescue his fate and told them everything that he knew about Kate and Damien.

Sitting in the café a few blocks away Sam and Justin went over the information that Maxime had given them.

Sam looked at Justin. His friend was still silent. Ever since they heard the news he'd hardly said a word.

"So, what's the deal?" Sam said. He glanced at the map and knew it would take an hour to just get out there, let alone find the house.

"Nothing."

"Right. So why the quiet act?" Sam asked.

"I don't know man. I think she fucked up. Bad."

"I think you're letting your imagination get the best of you. I mean she's in some serious shit, there's no doubt about that, but we'll find her and get her out."

"Yeah," Justin murmured. "It's just that... Man I don't even know... I just have a bad feeling about this."

Sam said nothing to that.

"Okay let's get moving," Justin said, and they both lumbered out of the café and walked towards their car.

Maxime got to the party house, swearing at himself. He'd missed the bus and had to hitch a ride out here. It took forever and now he feared he was too late. He walked into the house.

He recognized some of the faces, people he had partied with before. They were all passed out or asleep; it must have been a good night. Then he heard the wail from upstairs. The partiers barely stirred. Maxime got out his knife and slowly moved up the stairs. When he got to the top he could still hear sniffling. He took another step and the floorboard underneath his foot creaked.

Suddenly there was nothing but silence from the room. Damien took another look at his knife to make sure he was holding it tight. His sweaty hands were trembling too much for a proper hold. He heard some movement and looked up.

There was the quiet American with cold eyes in front of him with a gun pointed at his chest. Maxime instinctively dropped the knife. Kate's brother appeared around the same corner.

"You mother fucker." Justin reached out and grabbed Maxime by his collar and threw him against the door.

Maxime slammed against the ground and saw the big crazy American move in, hand cocked back for a punch. Maxime remembered what short work the psychopath had made of Damien in Amsterdam. He shielded his face and turned his head.

That's when he saw his friend. Damien. Lifeless. His head hung limp, his eyes open. Empty. Looking at the ground in front of Maxime.

"Damien?" Maxime stared and his face went white. He couldn't believe this was real. Damien was his best friend. They had been friends since they were kids. Raised in the bad parts of Marseilles, they'd lived off the streets, always relied on each other, always been there for each other, and now it was over. His friend lay there, so still, it scared him.

Maxime felt Justin's hand on his shoulder. He looked over to the big man and saw sympathy in his eyes. That surprised him.

"So what do you know man? We need to find who did this," asked Justin.

"All I know is Damien and Kate had stolen some drugs from their boss, and this was their final going away party before they left." Maxime's eyes darted at Sam who was scribbling down on a piece of paper.

"Who's this boss?"

They sat in the hallway for more than an hour. Maxime told them everything he knew about the boss. Sam stood by, writing everything down.

"So what do you do now?" asked Maxime.

"Us?" Sam asked. "You fucking kidding me? We find this guy and kill him."

Justin nodded grimly.

Maxime, shocked by the language, tried not to act like it affected him. "You're not going to the police?"

"Why would we do that?" Sam asked, giving Maxime a disgusted glare. "They probably wouldn't care, given the situation."

"I guess not." Maxime was still unsure if these two knew exactly what they were doing. "But do you know who you're messing with? It won't be easy to kill him. He's the biggest man in Nice. He's Russian mafia—"

"It doesn't matter, Maxime. We're going to do this no matter what..." Justin said.

"And me?" asked Maxime.

"Stay where you are. Don't let anyone know about this," Sam said. "Don't let them know that you even care. We'll need you to provide information for us, you understand?"

"Okay," Maxime was relieved that this was all that was being asked of him. He wanted revenge for his friend, but didn't have a stomach for physical violence. He looked at the two a lot more differently now. He still considered them crazy. But they were on his side now, and he was glad someone had such an appetite for violence. He looked at the one with the cold eyes. They still scared him, but not as much as before. He understood them more now.

"Just make sure you're not too obvious when you ask questions. We wouldn't want to lose you," said Sam.

"Of course not," replied Maxime. His concern seemed out of place. Though Kate's brother seemed to like him now, especially since they had both just lost someone close. The other one still seemed the same.

"Remember this and throw it away when you have it memorized, okay?" said Sam.

"Okay," Maxime looked at the paper. "I don't know when she'll come down?"

"Yeah, use it if you've been rolled up, and they're trying to get to us through you. We'll use it if the situation is the other way around. Of course that won't happen," said Justin.

"Why?" asked Maxime.

"Cause we don't get captured," said Sam.

Maxime wondered if the cold one was capable of any emotion.

CHAPTER 7

A stranger sipped his coffee, quietly taking in the bohemian neighborhood of *Vieux* Nice -the Old City. He'd been sitting at his table for the better half of a day. His glance at the street tangled up with someone else's stare. A woman at the bar initiated a conversation of the eyes. Physically she wasn't exceptional, but there was something about this woman that struck him the right way. All her mannerisms were confident. Her movements showed that she was sure of herself and knew what she wanted in life, others be damned. But he didn't dwell on it. He wasn't here to chase some woman. He was here to do a job. He looked away. She now entertained herself in a conversation with the bartender.

The stranger's eyes caught something down the alleyway. He folded his newspaper in his arm, threw the amount owed on the table and, without glancing at anyone, walked out the cafe.

The stranger hurried down the street, passing by tourists. His eyes were focused on a man in front of him. As he closed in on the man, he slowly took the slow unassuming demeanor of a tourist. He pretended to carouse through the card shop next to the man—his target.

The target was engrossed in a conversation with another large man, and was doing most of the talking. The target ended the conversation, sent the large man away, looked around, and walked through a door. It was a restaurant, one that the stranger already knew the target owned.

He walked around to the back of the restaurant where some garbage cans were sitting opened up in a dead end alley. Next to the garbage cans, a cook was seat, smoking a cigarette. The cook looked up and saw the stranger. There was no turning back now. The stranger walked up to the cook and gave his lost American tourist act. "*Bonjour, parle vous ingles?*" the stranger said and smiled.

"*Non,*" the cook said. He was giving the aloof Frenchman act.

That didn't deter the stranger. He showed the map to the cook and, still smiling, asked about a street name. The stranger knew that being nice and persistent rarely failed, regardless of culture.

The cook took the map and started to explain. The stranger kept saying "*oui*" to keep the cook's head down. All the while the stranger stole peeks at the back of the restaurant. He memorized the kitchen layout.

"*Merci, beau coup,*" the stranger said. "*Como vous se pelle vous?*"

"*Didier.*"

"*Je m'apelle Densm,*" the stranger said. It was an alias he frequently used. They shook hands, and the stranger bid Didier good-bye.

The stranger entered a small hotel located on the outskirts of *Vieux* Nice. The hotel faced a wide pedestrian street with an infinite flow of tourists. The stranger knew the walkway would provide an easy way to escape and disappear. He'd used stolen passports, from soldiers in Germany, to rent the hotel room.

"Hey Justin," the stranger said as he walked into the room.

Justin was sitting on a bed, cleaning weapons.

"Christ, put on the chain when you do that. What if the housekeeper walked in?" said the stranger. He'd already built a considerable amount of rapport with the housekeeper, a migrant worker from the Philippines who was eager for the meager tips he gave her. The stranger knew to keep things friendly. People were less suspicious of strangers who smile.

31

"She was already through here. So stop nagging me," Justin replied without looking up.

"Still, be careful." The stranger trusted Justin with his life. Their friendship grew in the fires of war.

"Yeah, I know Sam, I got it." Justin started to put the weapons together.

Sam flopped on the bed and let out a sigh. "A little testy aren't we?"

"Well, I know what I'm doing."

Sam stared at the ceiling, listening to his friend put the weapons back together. The sound had a soothing effect. A nostalgic nerve tickled, and though it wasn't from the best of times, it was familiar.

"Aayait man. Chill, my bad."

Justin didn't reply for a full minute. "So find anything new?"

"Yeah, I saw him."

Justin cocked his head slightly. "You're not messing with me are you?"

"Naw, it was him."

"Well?"

"Well," Sam said and propped up on both his elbows. "He appears to have a buddy of sorts."

"We already figured that," said Justice.

"Yeah, I know, he's like an errand boy. But he's a big motherfucker. Knows how to handle himself."

"Whatever. I'll knock his ass out. Anyone else?"

Sam paused and mentally grimaced. He didn't like it when Justin talked so bluntly. He always had to keep Justin in check, especially prior to missions. Justin just had extra energy. Sam rarely complained about it because when it came time to get things done, Justin would grab the focus needed and get it done. And Sam *knew* Justin would make short work of the target's friend. Justin was stout, thick as a tree trunk, and coiled with energy that could be summoned at a moment's notice. "No one we should worry about,"

Sam said. He searched his pants pocket for a cigarette, pulled out two, then threw one at Justin.

Justin lit his and threw his lighter at Sam. They inhaled hits of nicotine. For some reason he could smell old concrete. The hotel was falling apart.

"And his place?" asked Justin.

Sam took a deep drag from his cigarette hoping it would aid him in thought. "So far it seems it's the restaurant. Pretty accessible, but we need some better escape routes."

"Good deal. Do you think he has another place?"

"Probably. But we haven't the time to scope out another place. We'll just have to focus on this one." Sam waved and jabbed with his cigarette.

"I suppose."

"Don't worry. We'll stake it out long enough that he'll eventually swing by again."

"You think?"

"Yeah," Sam said taking another drag. "I think he'll hit it up again."

"We can't be dickin' around man. What if he gets spooked and goes somewhere else?"

"Remember he doesn't know we're coming after him. Things are quiet on his front. Why would he be expecting anything?"

"All right, so you picking up some French habits?" Justin gave a French accent, then imitated Sam's wave and jab with his cigarette.

"Screw you," Sam said, feeling more sensitive than normal. When Justin and he had first been to France they'd laughed at how the French would talk and wave their cigarettes like conductors of a conversation.

"You okay?" Justin asked.

"Naw, nothing. Just this woman I saw in the café. She seemed interested in me... as if she knew what I was doing."

"Did she say anything?"

"No, just looked."

"Ah, then fuck it. You're overreacting. Anyways, I told you your coffee recons would attract someone's attention sooner or later."

"Yeah, yeah I know," Sam said. He'd already decided it was the last time he'd do it.

"Besides I think you were turning French on me," Justin said and grinned. "Was she hot at least?"

"I was a second away from proposing."

Justin chuckled. "So let's check out the place. I'm fucking starving as is."

"*Vamanos* then," Sam said.

Justin put away the weapons, made sure they were locked in a suitcase, and followed Sam out. Once outside the hotel, they walked separately. They made their way towards the target's restaurant. First Justin stopped at a Chinese place for a quick bite.

Sam stood at a boutique staring at some of the most intricate carvings he had ever seen. The salesman hovered over Sam the moment he entered. The store was empty. One look at the prices and Sam saw why. Only a few things were under a thousand Euro.

Sam gravitated to a small dragon curling around a sphere. There was something about the eyes of the dragon that stilled him. He didn't know what it was or what it meant—he wasn't an art connoisseur—but he knew when he liked something. He bought it.

Gonna buy anything else? It was a text from Justice.

Sam stepped outside shaking his head so Justin could notice. Justin could eat a cow in two minutes flat.

u're nt in bsc anymo, enjy ur food. Sam texted back.

Coming out of the military Sam found that he had to force himself to slow down when eating. It all started in basic training where drill sergeants force privates to swallow their meals in a minute. Apparently Justin hadn't gotten the memo that he was out.

They got within range of the restaurant and started to window shop more, taking glances at the restaurant and its surroundings.

Goin dr at 4 o'clock, alone.

Sam saw the message, and turned to see Justin walking to a door. A few seconds later, Justin picked the lock and was in. Sam kept a visual guard of the door. His heart sped up.

Perfect view.

Sam looked around to see if anyone was paying attention to the apartment door. This was risky. If someone decided to enter that apartment there was no choice but to confront them, and that was the last thing they needed.

2nd exit through window, low vis.

Sam relaxed and moved on to another shop, constantly keeping tabs on the door.

Out, behind you.

Sam turned and noticed Justin rummaging through a head shop, not looking up, wearing a huge grin.

Wtf?

It's all good, more later.

"Damn. That was great," Sam said flopping back on their hotel bed.

"Well thank God we don't stick to your safe plans all the time eh?" Justin pulled out a cigarette and lit it up.

"Fuck you."

"The apartment, man," Justin said and lit up. He threw the pack and lighter at Sam. "That'll be our place to check everything out. It has a perfect view."

"Are you crazy?" Sam lit his cigarette and waited for the hit of nicotine to calm his nerves down. "How can you possibly think that's a good idea?"

"Ahhh, ye of little faith. That apartment is the best thing that could have happened to us."

"Okay, motherfucker. Explain what makes you think we can sit in that damned house. We're not going to start holding people hostage, and I know you're not thinking of asking really nice."

"Hey man you get more flies with honey, you know that?"

"Real cute,"

"Listen, it's an old lady's place, I saw her as she left and she was carrying a suitcase as if she was going on vacation."

"So?"

Justin raised his hand. "So when I went up the fridge was empty and there were several signs of an old lady going on vacation. For a long enough time that we can use it at our leisure."

"What kind of signs?"

"Ok, man, the lady had an itinerary printed out in the garbage. The flight heads out today," Justin said and grinned from ear to ear.

"Why didn't you just say that to begin with?" Sam leaned back and stared at the ceiling. "What about the neighbors, surely one of them would notice us going in?"

"Trust me, the ol' lady is a recluse, no one is going to try and visit, and didn't you notice that besides the shops there were no nearby windows with eyes on the door?"

Sam was about to question this claim, but decided to take his friend's word. "So, twelve hour shifts then?"

"Yeah, that's what I was figuring, starting at eighteen hundred. I'll go first."

"Yeah whatever tool. You mean six pm right?"

"Fuck you," replied Justin.

"Hey, it's not my fault you can't rise above your roots and not be a tool."

"Whatever," Justin said. "I figure a couple of days and we'll have enough info to make a plan." He glanced at Sam to make sure it was acknowledged.

"Sounds good," Sam said. He glanced at his watch. "You'd better go ahead and stock up on some food."

Justin grabbed his backpack, threw in some energy drinks, and headed out.

Sam glanced at his watch again. He wanted to go out and relax. And he had enough energy drinks and ephedrine to tough out his shift.

Justin waited for the lady to hand over the meal. She was moving exceptionally slow. He drummed his fingers on the glass counter so she could understand his haste. She in turn gave him an impatient look as if she couldn't be bothered. Justin grabbed the bag out of her hand. He rushed out into the street and headed for the apartment. He was glad they'd been blessed with the apartment find. He'd noticed the old lady out of the corner of his eye and didn't know why she piqued his curiosity, but he was glad she did. Surely this was a sign that things would go their way. He thought about Kate and an immediate rush of sadness hit him.

CHAPTER 8

J ustin grinned when he thought of his friend. Staring out the window at the Russian's restaurant was making his mind wander. He remembered when they'd first met. Sam had been new to the platoon in Iraq. A FNG: a fucking new guy. Unlike most other soldiers Sam was happy to be in Iraq. Though they weren't in the same squad, Justin kept hearing about how the 'new guy' would ask to go out on more missions. Sam would trade guard shifts with others in his platoon so he could leave the firebase and go on more patrols.

A grudging respect grew from that. Justin had been the most motivated soldier in the platoon. Now someone else was vying for the title. It wasn't competition. Rather they had something in common.

Then one day their platoon lost three guys to a mortar round. The soldiers were shuffled around and Justin found himself on the same team as Sam.

The first mission they did together was one that Justin would never forget. They were rolling in a convoy of five Humvees through Baghdad. Justin and Sam were together in the second last vehicle. It was a normally quiet neighborhood, so Justin wasn't especially alert. A flash and bang knocked the breath out of his chest. An IED, Improvised Explosive Device. Justin turned to see the last Humvee engulfed in flames.

It was immediately hit with a volley of withering AK fire from the top of a nearby building.

"Turn this fucker around!" Sam screamed at the driver. The driver just sat there. They had come to a stop, and the driver was frozen.

"Fucking turn it around," Sam yelled again. But the driver wasn't about to move.

Justin saw Sam take off. So he jumped out and followed. He knew that Sam was going to need some support by fire. So after a few meters, he took a knee behind a palm tree. It was horrible cover, but it would have to suffice. He lifted his SAW, Squad Automatic Weapon, and started firing at the top of the roof. He couldn't see anything but barrels and muzzle flashes. The enemy must have been firing blindly over the wall. It meant they would have to get lucky to hit anything. But they were sending so many bullets at the burning Humvee that it was only a matter of time.

Justin first squeezed the trigger for a twenty second burst. The SAW, a light machine gun with 5.56 bullets, spat out tracers and bullets at the building. Sam couldn't shoot through the cement wall, but he would be able to graze over them. Enough that their assholes would tighten and slow down their rate of fire.

Justin's bullets hit off the top part of the wall, and the enemy fire stopped.

It was long enough to allow Sam to sprint the last fifty open meters safely. When Sam got behind the flaming Humvee he took a knee facing the building where the shots were being fired.

"Set!" Sam screamed and started firing his M16 at the roof top.

It was a movement under fire that every infantryman knew by heart. Justin immediately got up and sprinted towards Sam, his heart racing and his head tight.

Sam's M16 had nowhere near the volume of bullets that the SAW had—even with the selector switch on three round bursts. The enemy started shooting again. As Justin got closer to Sam he heard a few bullets go by his head making a cracking sound. A few bullets hit the asphalt, spraying some gravel towards his face. He ran to a sitting halt next to Sam.

Aaron Grunn

"Fuck!" He brushed some of the gravel off his face. He was exhausted and sweat kept dripping into his eyes.

"Cover me, I'm going to get these guys out." Without hesitating for an answer Sam jumped into the still flaming Humvee and started to pull out the soldiers inside.

Justin started firing at the rooftop and the enemy stopped shooting again. Within a minute Sam had both the soldiers out. He pulled out gauze and tamped their wounds. They were both alive.

Crack! A bullet whizzed by Justin's head, followed by more bullets.

"Dammit!" yelled Justin. The enemy had picked up and moved to another building that had a better angle of Justin's position. Sam grabbed Justin and pulled him.

Just a split second later the spot where Justin had been kneeling was eaten up by a salvo of bullets.

Sam and Justin took up positions and started to fire back. It slowed down the enemy's fire, but didn't stop it. They fired back for a few minutes and were almost out of ammunition, when their convoy turned around and arrived to help. The fifty-caliber machine gun mounted on the top of the main truck started to rip through the top of the roof and in seconds it powdered into nothing.

The enemy fire stopped.

Sam and Justin got up and with two other guys from their team ran into the building and cleared it. They found four insurgents, bodies twisted and torn apart, on the roof.

Justin looked over at Sam and nodded his head. "You're a crazy one, eh?"

Sam gave a cold stare back at Justin then smirked. "I can see I'm in good company."

Justin chuckled again when he thought of that first ambush he had gone through with Sam. After that fateful day they were inseparable. Even after their missions they hung out.

Justin looked at the restaurant again. Still nothing. He tried to look through the curtains with binoculars again. Still nothing. No one seemed to be out tonight.

CHAPTER 9

Sam walked into the bar. It was quiet, unlike a lot of the pubs here in the *Vieux* Nice. He looked around. He usually liked Australian and British tourists. They were always a jovial bunch and great to hang out with, but tonight he wanted to be a stranger. Everyone appeared to be speaking French, perfect. Never a social butterfly, he liked the language barrier. It was something that kept him safe from his surroundings. It allowed him to observe as if he wasn't there at all. He always tried to detach himself from his environment, wherever he was. When it was done automatically it lifted a burden off his shoulders.

He walked up to the bar and ordered a beer. He took another look around as he sipped his brew. Most of the bar was broken into small groups around tables. All engrossed in their own conversation. No one paid him any attention. The clientele was older. He looked over the bar at which he was standing. It appeared the loners were grouped here. All hunched over their drinks.

Sam recognized Didier sitting at the other end of the bar. "*Bonjour,*" Sam said and sat down on the bar stool next to Didier. "*Didier, oui?*"

Didier gave Sam an annoyed glance. "Ya."

"Remember me? You gave me directions when I was lost. I'm Densm." Sam stuck out his hand and grinned.

"I remember... You find the place?" Didier asked.

"Yup, I did. Thanks a lot." Sam forced a smile and raised his glass of beer halfway in a toast to the favor. "So you speak English well."

"Yes, yes, I was an exchange student in America for a year."

"Really, where?"

"Ohio."

"I'm sorry."

Didier laughed. "It wasn't too bad."

"You kidding me? I've driven through that state, and I wanted to kill myself. I can't imagine living there."

Didier laughed again. "Yes I know, but it was okay."

"I suppose." Sam pointed at Didier's beer. "You must have drank and smoked a lot of ganj to keep sane."

"Yes, of course, what else is there?" Didier tried to smile then looked down.

Sam nodded his head. From this angle he could see some rivets in Didier's hands. Sam wondered how he got them. "Something got you down?"

Didier waved his cigarette. "My boss, he's an asshole."

"What's that?"

"Yes, he refused me raise. I've been working there for three years and nothing. He has money, but he doesn't want to give me any."

"Greedy bastard."

"I know this."

Sam ordered another round of beers. "To work," Sam said and raised his beer.

Didier raised his glass as well. "Work."

The two drank a few more rounds before Didier stumbled off with a murmur about having to wake up early.

Sam's head spun. A few too many toasts with Didier. He ordered a club soda. He was no longer a teen. Having his mind anything less than clear and sharp bothered him. Especially when he was alone. He drank it down, thinking about the girl in Tarifa. A sharp tremor ran through him.

Sam ordered another club soda. He could smell the perfume of all the beautiful women surrounding him. Another tremor ran through his chest. He shifted in his seat. He wondered if it was this mission that was making him nervous.

He felt someone's eyes on him. He glanced up. There she sat the other side of the bar looking him right in the eye. It was the same woman from the cafe earlier in the day. They stared at each other, both caught in the act. Someone bumped into Sam. It shook him out of his trance. He looked at the person who'd bumped him, then back at the woman. Her eyes were now down.

Sam could see why she caught his eye earlier. Her eyes emitted a mixture of wisdom and innocence. Her nose was slightly crooked, and there appeared to be a streak above her lip. She sported no makeup. Her summer dress highlighted her curves and made him feel tight in his skin. The physical beauty, however, wasn't what attracted Sam the most. It was the way she carried herself: a shy confidence of a woman who knew her sexuality.

Sam walked over to her. "Hi, my name is Sam," he put out his hand, his heart beating fast, glad his voice didn't crack. "Yours?"

"Adele," she said and shook his hand, letting it rest there for a second. "*Ashante.*"

"You keep staring like that Adele and I'll have to charge," Sam said. She stared at him for a second then smiled. He sat down next to her.

"So what were you doing today?" she asked.

Her question caught Sam off guard.

"What do you mean?" Sam said to buy time.

"At the cafe." Her eyes studied his face, "today."

Sam could see that she was genuinely curious about his behavior. "Reading," he lied, feigning a look of surprise. "Why?"

"No, you weren't." She twirled her light brown hair in her finger.

44

"Well I also like people watching," he said and paused to see her reaction. "It helps me think."

She turned away.

"So what about you?" Sam wanted to change subjects as quickly as possible. "What do you do here?"

"Well... right now nothing really."

Sam wasn't going to beg for information. It was up to her if she wanted to talk.

"It's a long story," she added.

Sam raised his eyebrows for effect. "What? You're shy now?"

He couldn't get enough of her eyes. Brown soft eyes. They seemed so welcoming, especially with that smile of hers.

"Well I... I've been here for a few months now." She waved her hand in a circle. "Figuring what I wanted in life."

"And?" Sam asked.

"I was part of *Medicins Sans Frontieres*," she said.

"For how long?"

"Just a few years."

"Why'd you stop?"

"My mother died a few months ago," she said and looked away for a second. "That's why I came back. My father, he needs me."

"Sorry about your mother."

"She had cancer for years." She stopped to take a sip of her drink.

"So how are you coming along?"

"It was pretty hard on my father. He really loved her." She moved closer to Sam.

"And you?"

"It's forcing me to think a lot about my life," she said.

"Did you not like what you did before?" Sam was studying her eyes now, seeing how they danced to his question. They flickered around, but stayed on his face.

"No I did, but sometimes... sometimes I felt that I should be doing something else. Something for me."

"I understand. I've been having some thoughts about what I do too."

"What is it that you do?"

Now it was Sam's turn to pause. The question caught him off guard, though he'd brought it upon himself. His normal style was to avoid the question. Or act hostile; that would turn people away. But what do you do when you can't use those options? All he'd done was, well it isn't something you talk about over a beer.

"Right now I'm vacationing with my friend, helping him out with a favor," he said. "Just checking things out, you know, what to do with my life and all." Sam waited for a few words but Adele seemed in a trance and ready to hear more. "I was in the Army for a few years," Sam said. Not that he would be heart broken, but he knew the anti-military streak that ran through a lot of Europeans and it would be a shame for this humanitarian to have that same tendency.

"Oh, that explains a lot."

"What do you mean?"

"You know very well what I mean." She smiled and gently poked his ribs.

"No, I really don't know."

"Oh of course not. Your mannerisms and scars." She traced her finger across the swirling dragon tattoo on his right arm, slowly stopping at each scar until she got to his shirtsleeve. "I love dragons, by the way."

Sam's heart raced to her touch. It was soothing yet electrifying, sending chills down his spine. "Badges of the trade."

"I understand," she said. Her face hardened. "I've been around war zones long enough to notice certain things."

Sam nodded his head. He glanced away to take in the bar. It was bustling. Yet the entire time he'd spent talking to Adele he thought it sounded dead quiet.

"Let's go for a walk," he said.

"Sure." She smiled.

They paid off their bills and walked out to *Vieux* Nice. A group of drunken students walked by. Through their loud slurred words, Aussie accents leaked though. Taking up most of the alleyway, and talking boisterously about their night's antics, they didn't pay any heed to Sam and Adele as they passed by.

Sam instinctively pulled Adele by the waist and brought her closer to him until the tourists passed by. Then they started walking down the street again, this time hand in hand. Sam felt the warmth of her hand and felt it travel to his heart.

Their conversation drifted to lighter things. Less about life altering thought and more about everyday mundane things.

They wandered around *Vieux* Nice, its maze of alleyways, dotted with pubs and cafes, before heading towards the *Promenade de Anglais*. It was early morning, but the promenade lay lit and a few tourists walked its spine. They moved down to the pebble beach and sat down.

In the distance lights of ships, lone beacons in the darkness of the ocean and sky, slipped by. The soft waves crashing on the beach provided a rhythmic lull. They sat in silence, enjoying the moment, each others' presence, the ocean, the breeze coming off it, and even the bohemian beach goers using the beach as a bedroom.

Sam looked at Adele, lay down on his back with his head resting on his hands, and stared at the sky. "I love this town... it feels so alive."

"I know. I was born only a few minutes from here. You know no matter where I've gone in the world I always loved it here the most." Adele leaned back on one elbow moving closer to Sam.

"Your parents from here?" Sam asked.

"Yes, my mother was a nurse, and my dad a fisherman." Adele stopped and looked Sam over. "I can still remember going to my father's fishing boat and heading out to sea. I felt like a great explorer. I love that feeling, you know?"

"That rush of the unknown... I live for it." He could smell her sweat, and feel the heat of her skin. Again he felt tight in his skin.

Adele smiled. "Yes. After I got my medical degree I joined *Medicins Sans Frontieres* and left Nice."

Sam listened and didn't want to speak.

Adele traced Sam's shirt with her free hand. "It was hard to leave, but I had to. My parents, they understood, but when I left I was so busy I hardly stayed in touch. I imagine that was hard on them. You know how parents are."

"No," Sam said.

Adele raised her eyebrows. "No?"

Sam wondered what she was thinking, but decided to go on. "No. My mother abandoned me when I was young. Never knew my father either. After that it was a string of saints for foster parents." Sam grinned, feeling embarrassed for some reason.

"Your mother, you never knew her? Her reason for leaving you?"

"She was a worthless cunt," Sam said and his eyes darted off to the ocean before returning to Adele to see how she would react.

"Of course, what woman leaves her son?"

Sam didn't smile, but he liked that she said that. "And yours?"

"I didn't stay in touch for years only writing cards every now and again. Then one day I received the news that my mother was extremely ill with cancer." She grabbed Sam's shirt.

Sam took her hand into his. Her honesty and willingness to open herself up gave him the chills. "Go on."

"I rushed back, but it was too late." Adele looked off into the dark sea.

"Adele, look at me." Sam's hand touched her cheek, moving her face so he could see her eyes. Lights glistened off them. He leaned forward and kissed her. He teased her with his lips on hers, before he pulled away.

"And your father?" Sam asked.

"He never said anything about it. That makes me feel worse. I'm his only child."

"Why? You were only following your heart. No one can blame you for that."

She looked into Sam's eyes. "My father still works. So I just try to help him around the house. He doesn't fish anymore, no money in that. So he ferries tourists around the French Riviera." Adele paused her hand tracing Sam's shirt. "He never lets me on the boat any more. I think he smuggles things too, but he doesn't want me to know about it."

"Everyone has to make ends meet." Sam stopped at that statement and looked off at the ocean and wondered how long this moment would last. He didn't know why, but he felt an ecstasy that he couldn't remember feeling before.

"Well, I have to figure out what to do with my life," Adele said.

Sam took in her words, and after some thought continued. "Why the rush? You have one life, might as well take your time trying to figure out what to do with it."

"I know, but it's hard when you have so much to think about it."

"Don't worry, it'll work itself out." Sam smiled.

Adele smiled back. "I spent most of my life giving and now I want to be able to live for myself. All my life was for other people, always, and now I want to deal with my own needs."

They sat absorbing each other's thoughts and the soft lull of early morning Nice.

"So what about you? I hardly know anything about you."

"Well," Sam trailed off. "You already know about my mother."

"Yes."

"After that I went from foster home to foster home..." Sam paused to absorb her reaction. "All worthless. When I was old enough to be on my own I became a gypsy."

"A gypsy?"

"Yes, just traveling around. Either holding menial jobs or selling drugs to get money."

"Really?"

"Yes, not all of us can be Mother Teresa." Sam smirked.

"Stop," she gave him a gentle pinch.

"But after a few years of that I realized I was going to wind up in jail or dead if I continued my ways. So I joined the Army to get myself straightened out."

"Did it work?"

Sam held back a laugh. "Yeah, I suppose."

"Why are you so scared?"

"What do you mean?" Sam felt jolted. He had dared to open up a little and was now wondering if she was going to attack him.

"Oh there we go again," she said. "I'm not going to judge you. I just want to know more. I trusted you. Why can't you do the same with me?"

"Well it just takes longer for me to open up, okay?" Sam murmured.

"Okay."

Sam almost smiled. A warm feeling crept up his chest.

"So why the Army of all things?" She asked.

"Well, I needed direction. It was also post 9-11, so I guess I had a patriotic surge. You know, wanting to be part of the fight for my country and all."

"So you were an idealist?"

"Yes, I suppose."

"You still idealistic?"

Sam let off a chuckle. "Naw, I was young and dumb back then. I think I believed in the inherent good of what I was doing. You know how it is when you're young."

"You don't believe anymore?"

"No. I when I signed up I actually thought it was for a greater good. I believed what our leaders said."

"You think they lied?"

Sam shook his head. "No, nothing so juvenile. Politicians are what they are."

"People who compromise their ideals."

"They may be fluid with their beliefs, but that's what's needed. The system wouldn't work otherwise." Sam wanted to change subjects. He didn't like talking about politics anymore. "But the biggest thing is I changed too much. I can't be idealistic anymore. I'm too calloused for that."

"That's sad." Adele slid her hand under his shirt and ran her fingers over his belly button.

"Why? I think naivety is a weakness, I'm glad I'm not naïve anymore."

Adele shook her head, "No naivety is beautiful. It is innocence, something we all have and need. Sam, I believe you still have some innocence somewhere in there." She circled her finger around his heart.

Sam grimaced. "Not in this animal."

"What do you mean, 'animal'?"

"I don't know, whatever." Sam looked away.

"Yeah you do," she said with a slight touch of anger in her voice, "don't pull that act."

Sam waited, hoping that maybe she would forget it and talk about something else, but her eyes didn't waiver. "Adele, I've done some horrible things in my life."

"In Iraq? Well that was war; you did what you had to. To get out."

"Yeah, but that's not it..." He thought of the consequences of telling a woman he just met the truth. "Sorry..." He would never be able to survive the blow to his self worth. "I can't, not yet."

"That's okay."

"Thanks." Sam looked at his watch and sat up when he remembered where he had to be. "Oh fuck! I've got to go, see my friend."

She looked at him inquisitively. "Go where?"

"My friend. I'm supposed to meet him in ten minutes."

"Why? What's so important all of a sudden?"

"Look," Sam replied. "He's a very good friend of mine. He was in Iraq with me... We've been through a lot together."

"His name?"

"Justin." Sam paused. "You know how I've never had any family?"

"Yeah."

"Well it means I have only had friends in my life and there's nothing more important than them, their loyalty, okay? There is nothing else in life that I trust more than that. We're supposed to meet for breakfast so that's what I have to do okay?"

"Yes," Adele said her eyes darting about on his face.

"Well I can't very well leave him high and dry, okay?" he looked into those eyes. "You understand?"

"Of course," she sighed.

Sam looked into those eyes as they accepted his answer in a resigned manner. He lifted a lock of hair from her face and moved in closer. He could smell her sweat. She didn't wear perfume; she didn't need to. He looked at her lips and kissed her. He could feel her warm body and pulled her closer, tasting her, smelling her, taking it all in.

Sam's phone went off and cut short what was about to transpire. He slowly pushed her off. "It's my friend," he said. "I have to go now."

Sam got her number and took off.

Adele watched as Sam sprinted away. She didn't know what to make of this escape. She still thought he was hiding something from her. But she felt something stir inside of her that she'd never felt before.

This excuse to run off seemed legitimate enough. The phone call proved that. He had been friends with this man in Iraq. A man who had fought along side with him. She looked around her. The beach was deserted at this time of the morning. She straightened her clothes out. She had to get back home. Her father would be worried.

When she got back, she walked in to find her father sitting at the table. His look was one of concern.

"Where have you been?"

"I'm not a child papa. I was out."

"I was worried."

"Sorry." She felt guilty for being so harsh with him. She loved her father and knew that he gone through a rough time when her mother died. "I met someone." She walked into her room without waiting for a reply.

Clement looked at his daughter as she walked off into her room. His pride and joy. She'd always been a little quieter than the other girls, more mature. When the others got boyfriends, she never did. He and his wife, Marie, let it slide as she was engrossed with schoolwork and volunteering her time to just causes. Their daughter the politician. Then she ran off to save the world. He hardly heard from her. When Marie was close to death he'd written Adele an urgent message. She came back, only a little too late. Marie had been so sad in her last days. What mother that hadn't seen her child in ages wouldn't be? She still couldn't understand why her daughter left a warm caring home for the cold hard world.

"Tell her I love her Clement, that I'm proud of her."

"I will Marie, just rest." She was on her last breath, and Clement hated to see his wife suffer. She passed away later that day.

Clement had tried to tell Adele, but knew it fell on deaf ears. His daughter was intent on making herself suffer. He'd never been angry at her, but he could feel the guilt eating her away. He tried to make it better, but she pushed him away. She was no longer his little daughter. No longer the same girl who held his hand as they walked the dock to their boat. He sighed as he thought of her. She was much quieter now.

Aaron Grunn

She had always been somewhat different. Now that she was back she was harder as well. She had seen too much of the bad side of man. Such things change a person. Clement knew; he had spent five years in Algeria fighting. He looked at his scars on his hands and arms. Most of his scars were physical; a lot of his friends weren't so lucky.

CHAPTER 10

"Where the fuck were you?" Justin shouted.

"Sorry man, I got caught up with some shit."

"What shit?"

"A chick man."

"Oh." Justin grinned and raised his eyebrows. "So how was she?" He elbowed Sam in his ribs. Justin was surprised. Sam rarely seemed moved by women. He wondered what kind of girl does that to such a cold man.

"Oh fuck, nothing like that," Sam replied. "But she's pretty cool." Sam grinned then quickly suppressed it. "You know, whatever."

"Uh-huh. You fucking falling for some bitch ain't ya Sam?" Justin said. "You didn't tell her what we were doing did you?"

"Are you fucking kidding me?" Sam retorted. "Do I look like some retarded high school kid that falls in love after one fucking day? Do I have bubble gum in my mouth? Have I ever done something so stupid as to jeopardize anything for some cunt?"

"My bad, my bad, Jesus fucking Christ. I was only asking." Justin raised his hands, then started to pack his things up. "Besides if you weren't fucking falling for her, you'd only have said 'no'. The fact that you snapped shows that you must really be in fucking love with this fucking bitch." Justin looked up with a mischievous look on his face.

"Get the fuck outta here with that Freudian couch bullshit. I am not falling for some bitch, so just drop it."

"Why? I'm hitting a nerve ain't I?"

Sam laughed. "You fucking cunt. You ain't hitting a god damned thing. So go fuck yourself."

"Man... I'm good."

"So cunt, did you see anything?" Sam sat down.

"Well I saw him," Justin replied while zipping up his bag. "And he came in around midnight."

"Then?"

"Then he walked in, talked to some guy on the wait staff, walked upstairs and went to sleep."

"Nothing else?"

Justin thought for a second. "Not really man. That restaurant must be absolutely clean because I don't see anything illegal going down at all. I mean nothing out of place whatsoever. Oh yeah... and he appears to be pretty arrogant."

"How so?"

"Well he walks like a man who owns the streets and not someone being hunted."

"So at least he doesn't know anyone is coming after him."

"Exactly." Justin nodded his head.

"Good deal we should be good. If we figure out his pattern even get a rough estimate we should go ahead with it," Sam gave his friend a nod indicating he was set.

"Yeah almost definitely, I say one or two more shifts tops and we should be set," Justin agreed and walked out.

Sam turned to the window and looked at the restaurant. This was going to drag, especially after time flew with Adele. Not to mention he hadn't slept in more than a day.

But he didn't care about that. He cared about her. He'd never felt this way before and it was eating him up inside. All the small doubts he'd been having with his chosen path in life had come up when he saw her and had been chewing away at him ever since. It made him angry with her. That she had caused such happiness, self-

56

loathing and introspection at the same time. Her beauty had been a great contrast to the ugliness he felt inside.

He glanced back at the street. Still trying to pull guard, not wanting to get too lost in thought, Sam looked around again. The restaurant was busy. People milled around. None of them looked like the target.

His thoughts drifted back to Adele. Here he was; he'd never fallen for a woman before. Now here he was about to tell her everything, for what? A feeling? He had known her for one night. How many times had he laughed at some of his friends for feeling the same thing after a short while? And slowly his thoughts drifted to the girl in Tarifa. Then to Iraq. And he closed his eyes, the sewer smell of Baghdad coming back to him, and the shouts, and the screams.

The building in East Baghdad was the main hit that night. Sam and Justin's squad were clearing it. Everything went amiss from the start. As they kicked off the raid with a shotgun blast to the lock, gunfire hit the outer door. They pulled back and returned fire. Unfortunately Curt, who had been point man, was shot right through the neck. The medic immediately attended to him.

They still had to go in. So when their squad leader yelled, their support by fire increased their shooting. When the enemy stopped firing the squad ran into the compound. Sam took point man, while Justin took second. They made it to the front door without any casualties. They kicked down the door and ran in.

It was pitch black inside, so they turned their flashlights on. They cleared the first floor then went for the stairs.

That's when things got worse. The squad leader called in the support by fire to stop firing, as they'd been peppering the second floor the entire time.

"Frag!" someone yelled.

They all hit the floor when they heard the call, and a grenade came tumbling down the stairs. It went off instantaneously. Sam had been staring right at it and was caught off guard.

He should have died. But Justin grabbed him and threw him behind some cover.

The grenade went off and all were hit by the concussion. When they got up and started to check each other they saw two guys down: Mike and Tom.

They were still moving, but it didn't look good. The squad leader called for the medic and told everyone else to stack up.

It seemed heartless to move on, yet they had to clear the second floor. If they didn't, they risked getting more casualties.

They all started shooting upstairs, through the door, the walls and the ceiling. Anything their bullets penetrated they shot. The house wasn't well built so their bullets were able to go through most of the walls.

Walking as fast as possible they moved up the stairs. Sam's heart was pumping. His flashlight gave away his position, and he felt like a sitting duck. But he felt better since Justin was right behind, covering him.

The second floor really wasn't anything but a small hallway with a door leading to the roof. The door was barely hanging on by the hinges. At the top of the stairs were some boxes in the hallway, but nothing big enough to hide a person.

All who had a clear view of the second floor were still firing. The squad leader yelled for ceasefire.

As Sam approached the door, Justin instinctively moved besides him and with nothing more than a glance and a nod they pulled it open.

Sam moved through the opening and turned right.

Sam knew the main ingredients to successful room clearing were speed, surprise and violence of action. The last one was the most important. If he became more violent than his enemy and he had the upper hand. If he failed at this task he'd lose. In this game of "you bet you ass" that was the difference between life and death. This wasn't something that Sam or his squad was missing. Neither was the speed; they'd worked together enough to move like water through a building. Surprise was currently their main problem. They'd regained some of it by hitting the second floor with a barrage of bullets. But for all they knew, the enemy could have hidden behind some cover and been waiting for them.

All this raced through Sam's mind as he hooked right into the dark room. Adrenaline was pumping though his bloodstream in anticipation of what was about to go down.

Sam turned and caught one man in the beam of his flashlight. The man was obviously just recovering from the assault. His AK 47 was in hand, and Sam wasn't going to take a chance. Sam fired into the man's chest. Usually a pair of bullets was enough. Sam, however, knew this was never the case. He always shot until the person dropped. With 5.56 bullets it usually took more than a few to drop a man.

Four shots to the chest made the man stumble a little, but it wasn't enough. Sam was still walking towards him. Sam raised his rifle slightly and shot through the man's head. The man fell. Sam walked up to the next corner scanning the rest of the room until he saw Justin. There were three insurgent bodies in the room, ripped and twisted from the gunfire. Cracked bone pierced through skin, and seemed artful.

Sam focused on the middle of the room where he could hear some shuffling. There was a woman cowering over her son. They seemed untouched. Sam walked over to her to search her and make sure she didn't have any weapons.

She gave him a look of utter hatred. Sam didn't blame her. They'd come to her home and put her family in danger. But he felt no remorse. The man of the house was to blame for putting his family in jeopardy, not the soldiers.

The woman looked around, Sam scanned around as well and his light went over a small lump. He looked at it again and a cold wave splashed over his body.

The woman screamed and rushed over to the lump.

It was a young boy. He'd been hit in the back of the head with a bullet and what replaced his face was a gaping hole. Spilled all around him were remains of his face and brains. The mother held her son and screamed at the soldiers.

Sam watched the restaurant, the image of the young kid bright in his mind. Whenever there was too much time to think, the image would come back and fester. It looked like strawberry and whipped cream had spilled from the child's head. Sam sighed, and shook his head trying to shake his thoughts off. He stared at the restaurant and thought of the mission.

Their main plan was to take out the target by more barbaric means. Justin had a knife he'd been keeping sharp. It was the same one he had in Iraq. Justin was the only person Sam knew who had a confirmed kill with a knife.

Justin had pulled it out one day when his SAW jammed face to face with an insurgent. Sam had been five feet behind and was raising his weapon. But just when he was about to yell at Justin to drop, Justin had pulled out his knife. With one hand Justin slapped the Iraqi's AK down and with the other, slashed his throat. He then proceeded to slam his SAW's butt stock to his head to finish the man off.

Justin was a violent man. He had reacted so quickly that day even Sam had been amazed. It was always good to have a person like that for a friend.

CHAPTER 11

Pyotr munched on a croissant and sipped on his coffee. Things hadn't been going well lately. Business hadn't been bad, but it could be better. Then there was Damien and that girl he had to kill. He couldn't believe it. He had treated the boy like a son and taken care of him. Shown him the ropes and let him rise in their group relatively quickly. Then Damien went and betrayed him.

He shook his head. They had been madly in love. Even in their last moments they had been true to each other. The kind of love even Pyotr knew was special. It pulled at his heartstrings for its purity. They had let that love take over their minds. Feeding off its ecstasy they brushed away any rational thought. Foolish kids. So much potential, so much talent, thrown away for a feeling.

"Baby, let's rob that shipment when it comes in." Kate was lying in bed with Damien. Both naked and covered with sweat, side by side, Damien behind her, his arms over and under her.

He took a deep breath. He loved Kate, she was the most amazing girl he had ever met, but she had some crazy aspirations. With her nudging he'd been skimming more than he had in the past. Selling without even letting his boss know. Getting a few deals on the side and not telling anyone. So far nothing bad came from it. This, however, was on another level. He let her go and rolled on his back. "I don't know baby, sounds a little risky." He said this through a clenched jaw. Partly because he was tense about the topic, but mostly because he was still recovering from the beating Kate's brother had laid on him.

It had been a pretty big shock when her brother had gotten a hold of him back in Amsterdam. He'd noticed that Kate's brother had been giving him the evil eye their entire time there. Kate reassured Damien it was just the protective brother playing a role. But when that first fist caressed Damien's face, he knew different. Her brother was a psychopath. Kate blamed the war for changing Justin. Damien, still in love and wanting her to stay, agreed and forgave her. She promised that he would never have to see her brother again and that was good enough for him. Nevertheless the pain lingered.

"No not at all," Kate said and rolled over to face Damien. "You know where the exchange is going down right?"

Damien grinned. Her mind was grinding away at another idea. She'd probably been thinking about a plan ever since his friend had mentioned something about the deal. His friend had come to him last week and mentioned how the boss had gotten a new connection for cocaine. The first exchange was going to go down in a few days. It would be approximately fifty kilos for a relatively cheap amount. His friend was pretty talkative and divulged on exactly when and where it was all going to happen. "Yes, but," again he paused. He was still unsure about this whole thing and he felt uncomfortable even talking about it. Life was good, why did she want and go rocking the boat? It was that American energy she had in her. The same energy he loved.

"But what babe?" She moved in closer. "We know where it's all going down. It's a first time exchange so no one really trusts each other. When anything goes wrong they'll probably blame each other and end the relationship at that. We just have to be smart and not get caught. I bet it won't be that hard to find a weakness in their defense."

"Yeah, I suppose," Damien said. As usual Kate was winning him over with her calm analysis. He looked her over then settled on her eyes and waited for her plan.

"It'll be easy baby." Kate stroked the healing scars above Damien's eye. "We know when and where it's going down, so all we do is go down to Le Port early. Obviously there'll be guards around the boat, but a distraction will get rid of them. Then when they're distracted, we'll go inside and take the drugs!" Kate gently pressed on Damien's scar, took a breath and eagerly waited for Damien's answer.

"Sounds great baby." Damien smiled and looked her in the eye. He knew that she had given him an over simplified version of the plan. He was certain that she probably had planned it to the most minute detail like she usually did. She had a knack for using her imagination and coming up with outlandish yet sane plans. "Sounds absolutely great." He leaned in and kissed her.

That's why he loved her so much; she was full of energy and not boring like so many other girls he had met. That sparkle in her eye as she came across an idea. He bit her lip. She'd been right so far, and he was sure that she would be right again. She had a knack for these things. He kissed her again and rolled on top of her. Kate giggled and wrapped her arms around him.

"What will we do with all the money?"

"I always wanted to go to Bali." Kate licked one of his scars with the tip of her tongue and softly touched his face.

"Where is that in Indonesia?"

"Yeah... Indonesia. I heard it was beautiful out there. We could go to the main island or some smaller island... there're plenty to choose from. And with all our money we can buy our own island."

"Indonesia sounds good, but I don't think we can buy our own island baby. Maybe our own beach."

"Then that's where we'll go, Indonesia," Kate said and giggled. "We'll buy some land next to the ocean so we can dock our boat right next to where we live. We can have a little farm with cattle and we can grow pot."

"Oh yes? So we will become beach bums or farmers?"

"Both baby, we'll be beach bums with a farm, but the locals will know us as farmers. We have the boat, so we can go wherever we want, whenever we want. No one will ever think of coming out to Indonesia to find us, and when they do we'll just sail away."

Damien nibbled on her neck. "What else?"

"We'll smoke the finest stickiest weed and fuck all day on the beach."

Damien didn't answer. They embraced in a long kiss. More passionate kisses followed and their embrace slowly became more rhythmic. Their bodies moved as one, rogue lovers lost in each other.

Pyotr opened up the day's newspaper. He glanced at the headlines. Not much was going on in France. Not anything that would affect business at least. He noted that the insurgency in Iraq was picking up. He didn't care too much for Muslims, and wished the Americans the best in their adventures. More importantly, he saw that the police hadn't made much progress in the investigation of a double murder involving an American tourist and Frenchman.

That was good. His own boss had been furious when he had heard about the murders, as it brought about unnecessary attention. The last thing they needed was the police sticking their snouts in their business.

Pyotr didn't like his boss, Fyodor. Another problem to fester in his mind. Fyodor put up with Pyotr since he brought in money. Fyodor hadn't been angry at the fact that Pyotr murdered two young people, but rather that he made it a point to display them. It was because of this that the police had been scrutinizing all the organized crime in the area.

"More coffee, Pyotr?"

Pyotr looked up at the waitress. Shaken from his train of thought, he looked at her for a second. She was Polish, extremely hard working and beautiful in her own way.

"Of course Magda, please." He smiled and took the fresh cup of coffee from her. "Thank you."

She smiled back at him.

The fallout after the drugs were stolen had been severe. The Haitians were certain that he'd been behind it all. He had to convince them afterwards that he had no idea what was going on. A potential lucrative partner almost turned into an enemy. The gruesome killings helped Pyotr's standing with the Haitians infinitely. Rene, the Haitian leader, wouldn't have respected Pyotr if he hesitated to kill those who betrayed him. Now they were back in business.

He glanced at his watch. It was late and Aleksei wasn't anywhere to be seen. Pyotr took another sip of coffee. He was worrying too much. He should just enjoy this. The Haitians had promised more and more cocaine. If the last shipment was any hint of things to come things were going to be very good from now on.

CHAPTER 12

Hey man, reconn restarant. Justin sent a text to Sam. His head was spinning, and he couldn't stop thinking about his sister.

Justin walked in the restaurant and looked around. It was empty except the waitress behind the bar and a man behind a newspaper. He sat on a stool. The waitress came over to him and asked what he wanted.

"*Bonjour*," Justin said. "Uh, a coffee please."

"Of course," beamed the blond waitress. She turned around and started to brew one.

Justin was surprised by her fluent English, and the curves beneath her clothes. He took another look around and froze in recognition of a face. The man behind the newspaper was looking up at him. It was the target. He got up and walked towards Justin.

"You American?" The target extended his hand and smiled.

"Yeah man." Justin's thoughts were racing would this hurt the mission? Justin figured the only thing he could do now was to go full on with the American tourist role. He grasped the target's hand enthusiastically. "The name's Pat."

"Pleasure to meet you. Mine is Pyotr." He looked over Justin. "What brings you to our fair city?"

"Oh, just here on vacation, soaking some sun." Justin's anger was swelling in his chest. Here was the man who killed his sister. Here was his chance to kill him. There was no one in the restaurant besides the waitress. The alley to the front door was empty. He could very well get away with it. Just grab Pyotr and pound his face until he stopped moving. But he wouldn't get away. The mission was important since he could get away with it.

"Very good. You having a good time?"

"Oh yes, a beautiful city," Justin said. This man, who he wanted to kill, was strangely pleasant. "Beautiful girls too." He nodded his head over to Magda.

"Of course." Pyotr grinned as Magda walked over with the coffee. "She's very beautiful."

Magda looked up with a shy smile, brushing hair from her face.

"This one on me," Pyotr said. He looked at the doorway where Aleksei now stood. "And now I must leave." Pyotr put his hand out again. "Enjoy your time here Pat." They shook hands, "I hope to see you again."

"Hopefully, take care, and thanks." Justin watched as Pyotr and his right hand man walked out.

The other man was big, very big. But Justin had taken out bigger men before. His level of intensity usually out did everyone. Pyotr looked a lot scrawnier than Justin had imagined; he would be easy to take down.

But Pyotr had been terribly friendly. Justin couldn't wrap his mind around that. It wasn't a sort of fishy friendliness. It was a genuine warmth. Not what he had expected from the man who murdered his sister.

Kate. Again she flashed before him, and the sympathy he felt for Pyotr dissipated.

He looked at Magda and sipped on his coffee. She wasn't gorgeous, but had a nice body. She caught him staring and blushed.

"He's a good man." Justin indicated towards the door through which Pyotr had left.

"Yes, a very nice man."

Justin looked at the stairs leading up to the second floor. "Toilet?"

"Yes, up the stairs and to the left."

Justin walked up and saw the bathroom door to the left. He noticed the other door to the right. He tried it but it wouldn't open. He tried moving it a little. It wasn't rock solid, a little muscle, probably a swift donkey kick, would take it down. The hallway had a window, but was otherwise empty. He looked in the bathroom: not big enough to hide a person. He walked back down the stairs.

As he came down, he caught Magda taking another look at him. Justin smiled and walked up to her. "So when do you get done with work?" Justin always beat straight to the bush. She wasn't as beautiful as he had initially thought. Her lips were thin, and her face seemed a little lopsided. But her body was curvaceous and her movement was highlighted with an unknown factor that tickled his cock.

"At two."

"How about we meet outside the *Cathedrale Ste-Reparte* at two thirty?"

"Okay," Magda said, blushing beet red.

Justin nodded and walked out.

THE REASON

*L*e *Port* was a sight at night. Flanked on two sides by restaurants, and opened to the Mediterranean Sea on the other. It was quiet and void of tourists.

In a dark corner of the port, Kate and Damien kissed each other.

"Ready babe?" Kate asked with a little anxiety in her voice. This was a scary undertaking and she needed to see confidence in Damien's eyes.

"Of course," Damien said. "We're going to be fine baby."

"Okay baby." They kissed again. "I love you."

"I love you too," whispered Damien.

They'd gone over the plan, between love making sessions back at Damien's place. They even managed to come out here a couple times to double check on the location of the boat.

Surrounded by all the beauty of *Le Port* the men on *Le Lumiere* couldn't feel much love for the place. The four of them had been stuck on the boat for three days guarding a valuable shipment.

Louis was the team leader. He'd been given this job because he was a trustworthy man. His boss, Rene, had taken him aside and told him he was the only man for the job. Louis had been excited about it then, happy he was going to have a chance to prove himself. But now he seriously doubted those words. Who would take off with fifty keys of cocaine? The job hadn't been too hard. Sail in and dock. All their papers were in order; their suitcases were well hidden and properly insulated. Then they sat and guarded until they bled boredom.

Louis watched Clement-Marie and Clement-Baptiste walk away to get some food and glanced around the port again. Gerald was sitting against the rail falling asleep. The deal was going down with half a million Euros being paid for the cocaine. His cut of that would be around a tenth of that. Then he would have to pay the rest of the crew. Not much for himself and his family, but he was slowly working his way up. His time would come.

In the distance he could see a couple locked in an embrace. Louis sat down and lit a cigarette. A few more hours and they could be on their way. Louis drifted off listening to the lull of the nearby cars, the rocking of the boats. He stared at the reflection of the restaurants off the water. The smell of the sea was clean here. It was the only thing he liked.

Louis was pulled out of his trance when he noticed the car in front of him on fire. He stared at it for a second, jolted, not sure what to do. He hit Gerald on the shoulder to wake him up. Suddenly he heard the sirens and saw flashing lights coming down the street. Gerald moved around uneasily. Louis felt just as unsure about what to do.

"Don't do anything Gerald," said Louis. "Just let it burn out. It's not our problem."

Gerald nodded his head, his eyes still half open.

A police car parked in front of them, and two policemen jumped out, walking over to the burning car. Whatever had been set on fire was dying out. A policeman stomped the base of the fire then used his jacket to put out the remaining flames. Louis tried to remain as still as possible. He was in the shadows of his boat. If he remained motionless, the police wouldn't notice him and wouldn't bother him. A young man came up to them and start talking and pointing towards Louis. The police looked right at their boat and headed towards him. Louis jumped off onto the dock and beckoned Gerald to follow him. He walked up to the police and smiled.

"Assholes!" The young man yelled, pointing at Louis. Slowly but surely Louis told them exactly what he'd seen.

The policemen walked Louis over to car's front right wheel. The remains of a melted and charred glass bottle lay right behind it. One of the police picked up a charred piece of plastic with the remains of a wire attached to it.

Louis felt a tickle in his toes that spread to his gut and churned them into knots. When he'd first seen the fire he'd forced himself to believe it was possible for a car to spontaneously combust. Now that he saw this initiator, he knew otherwise.

Louis looked back at the boat. No body was on it. A small crowd had initially formed, but was now dissipating. He looked at Gerald who was still talking to the police, not concerned with the boat. The loud young man who had made the scene was nowhere to be seen either.

When the police left Louis walked back to the boat as quickly as possible, Gerald following. Louis jumped in and hopped inside the cabin. He looked at the suitcases. He looked around the cabin. Nothing out of place. Gerald, standing in the doorway, gave him a puzzled smile. Louis shook his head and smiled.

As Louis walked out, his arm brushed up against the side of the door and he felt something wet. He looked down, puzzled by the sensation. The puzzlement ignited his paranoia. He looked down and saw small puddles of water on the floor. He rushed over to the suitcases, opened one, and he was hit by a rush of blood to his head. The empty suitcase laughed at him.

Just half an hour ago things were looking great. He was going to go back home with some money and some respect from his boss. Now, he felt another bout of weakness in his stomach as he thought of what would possibly happen next. He stumbled out side, leaned over the rail and spewed out his guts.

Louis remembered watching Rene pour boiling water on a man's testicles for lying. Louis knew as the leader he would be taking all the blame. At best Rene would think Louis was incompetent and kill him quickly. Rene hadn't shown himself to be a person who put up with much room for error. Louis couldn't run. That would get his family killed. All he could hope for was his family to be spared. And a quick death.

Louis looked at the bile slowly floating away. He would soon be a pile of slush floating in the Caribbean.

Kate was in the dimly lit part of the port. She slid in the water and took of all her clothes except her swimsuit. She had a four rubber bags tied to her wrist. An all-state swimmer back home, it took her less than one minute to swim the seventy-five meters to the boat. She paused next to the boat's hull as she waited for her signal.

She saw the light from the fire flickering off the boat's hull. Then sirens sounded. A minute passed and the police arrived. She heard Damien yelling and blaming the men on the boat. Kate laughed silently at her lover's acting ability.

"Assholes!"

She grabbed the rope for the anchor and climbed up the boat. Luckily, there wasn't much light, and all the focus was around the car. Still, her heart pounded and felt like it was in her mouth. She snuck inside the cabin and saw the suitcases.

She unsheathed a diver's knife and pried them open. She stabbed one bag with her knife and took a snort. She was going to need the added energy for the swim back. It didn't take long for it to hit her bloodstream. She pulled out the four rubber bags and stuffed them with cocaine. She tied them, making sure there was enough air trapped inside so they would float.

It was heavy, but with the extra energy from the snorted line, she carried it outside. She lowered the bags into the water making sure they didn't splash. She slid in and swam away.

Damien and Kate kissed. They looked at each other one last time gathering the strength for what they were about to do. They each turned around and walked in opposite directions.

Damien went towards the north side of *Le Port*. He wore small backpack and carried a brown bag in his left hand. As he rounded the corner, he saw the boat with the two men. He slowed his pace down and noticed that one was asleep. The other was looking westward, lost in thought.

Damien knelt down next to a car, pretending to tie his shoe and placed the brown bag behind the front wheel. He pulled the wire antennae out, peeled off the tape at its end and stuck it to the tire. He glanced out of the corner of his eye to make sure he hadn't been seen. As he left, he pulled out his phone and let the police know what was happening. Twenty yards away he took out a car remote control and pressed a button.

Pressing the button sent a signal to the device underneath the car. The initiator was a receiver from a remote control car. The press of the button of the RC car's controller completed an electrical circuit in the initiator, causing a spark. The spark started the fuel which was a gasoline mix similar to napalm. It lit up setting off a low level explosion. No shock wave, just enough to get the tire and everything underneath the wheel well burning. Damien waited for the police.

Damien walked away from the police as they chatted with the two Haitians. He moved away from the light. He took a seat on the edge of the port and waited.

Kate swam up to him, in obvious strain. He looked around to make sure nobody was watching before helping her up. He handed her a small bag with some clothes to put over her one-piece bathing suit.

The bags were heavy. He grabbed three of them and let her carry one. They walked back to their car, parked no more than a block away, throwing the bags into the trunk.

Damien jumped in the drivers seat and started up the car. He put the car in first gear then shifted it back into neutral. His heart beat against his ribcage. He looked over at Kate and saw the same tension on her face. He grabbed her, and they locked lips. He pulled away and smiled.

"You okay baby?" Damien asked.

"I'm beat," she said. "You were great babe. You gave me all the time in the world."

"No you were great." Damien kissed her again. "Only you could pull fifty kilos of weight over a hundred meters of water." He shifted the car into first gear and released the emergency brake. He pressed on the gas, released the clutch, and they were off.

Kate grabbed a towel from the back and dried her hair out.

In the trunk the fifty kilos of cocaine shifted as the car turned. Damien knew where to sell it. He could sell it in a day or two at about ten grand a kilo. That would pull in half a million. They could be a little more patient and sell it for around thirty grand a kilo, in smaller units. It would take closer to a week for that, but it would be worth it. Damien was certain what they had was pure cocaine. It would be a cinch to sell it all. Marseilles was a big market and he knew people out there. He just had to make sure not to make any waves while doing so. He got on the A8 and pressed the accelerator until the little car couldn't go any faster, hundred and sixty kilometers an hour, fast enough to get away, not fast enough to attract attention on the French Freeway.

He looked over at Kate. She was curled up on her seat, passed out from exhaustion. Her eyes shielded from the lights of cars they passed. Damien reached in the back for another towel and covered her. They'd done it. Together. As they would be until the end. Damien looked ahead at the road, all that nervousness from before turned into elation. He looked over at Kate with a sense of pride; her plan had been perfect.

CHAPTER 14

Justin walked down to the northern edge of *Le Port*. His phone vibrated again. It was Sam. Justin hesitatingly answered it.

"Did it go smoothly?" Sam asked

"Yeah, walking around *Le Port* right now," Justin said, emphasizing the French accent on the '*r*'.

"Oh... You good?"

"I'm fine."

"Sure?"

"Don't worry... I'm good."

"All right. I'll talk to you later."

"Yes, later." Justin hung up the phone. He'd walked upon a blackened part of concrete made from a burn. They hadn't even bothered to clean it up. Justin looked at the burn mark. It was weathered away, except for some melted glass.

Kate.

Justin covered his eyes as tears poured forth. The image of his sister was seared in his mind. His body shook for a moment, then after a few minutes the tremors died down. He got up and walked away from *Le Port*. It was too much for him. He hailed a taxi over and headed back to the hotel.

"He hasn't returned since he left in the morning." Sam was briefing Justin on his mind-numbingly boring shift. "You look pretty fucking exhausted." Sam saw marks on Justin's neck. "Uh oh, who's the lucky lady?"

Justin grinned. "Some Polish bitch. Met her for lunch then took her back to the hotel."

"You do her dirty, Justin?"

"You fucking know it, man."

Sam laughed. "Good deal," he said and grabbed his bag. "So you feeling better now?"

"A lot."

Sam waited for more to come out of his friend. He was sure sleeping with the Polish chick was therapeutic, but it was a mere band-aid on a wound that needed more than that. "You sure man?"

"Yeah, Sam."

Sam waited again. He really didn't know how to go about this. Life was a lot easier when you didn't care. "If you ever need to talk about it, you know, I'm here."

"Right." Justin looked at Sam with a sad smile.

"Seriously Justin... sometimes it's better to talk about things like this. You let it fester and it can eat you up."

"This coming from the poster child of cool and reserved?"

Sam took the jab in stride; there were more important things at stake. "I'm just saying... I love you bro, and if you need me I'm here."

Justin had been emptying his bag and stopped for a moment. "I know Sam. I never had any doubts about that. Ever."

Sam nodded in acknowledgment. He pushed his hands in his pocket, yet again unsure on how to proceed. "I can't imagine how you feel about... you know... Kate, so if you want to talk about it..."

Justin turned his gaze from his bag and looked at his friend. "I miss her a lot man. Like there's this big hole in me. You know?"

"Right man."

"And I don't know what else to do but kill this Russian."

"We'll get him Justin. Don't worry about that... we'll fucking end him." Sam stepped to Justin and placed his hand on his shoulder.

"Damn Sam," Justin said, flashing a grin. "That French whore softening you up?"

"What ever man." Sam took his hand back. "I'll never change for some woman."

Justin shook his head. "Do what you gotta do, Sam."

Sam nodded his head at his friend's response. "I'll talk to you later." As he left, he pulled out his phone and called Adele's number. It rang twice and a man picked up.

"*Oui?*"

"Is Adele there?"

The man on the other end hesitated. Sam wondered if he had the wrong number.

"One second... please," Clement replied.

CHAPTER 15

They met in a teashop, a block from the beach. Sam was already sitting down to a cup of coffee, not tired, but having gone without sleep for more than forty hours, he knew he would have to hit an eventual wall, and he waited for it with trepidation. He also knew, despite his words to Justin, that he wanted to see Adele. For some reason he couldn't stop thinking about her.

The dimly lit Scottish teahouse wasn't, unlike most French cafes, filled with a cloud of cigarette smoke.

When Adele moved in for a kiss, Sam pulled away just as their lips touched. He held her at half an arms length and examined her face. He pulled a chair for her. Though she gave him an inquisitive look, she took a seat. She ordered a coffee, and they sat in silence until it came.

"So, was your friend okay?"

Sam saw the twinkle in her eyes. He could tell that she was prodding him for another answer. "He'll live." He smiled back. "Perhaps we should take a walk?"

Adele nodded her head non-noncommittally and looked at her coffee. "You like walks huh? Let's go back to my place."

They walked in silence until they arrived at her place. Sam stood in the middle of their living room smelling the cement and perfume in the air. As she started to ask him a question, he grabbed her by her arm. He looked at her face. He could smell her sweat, and as he could feel her soft skin. He moved closer, and opened his mouth to speak. He wondered if he was really going to tell her.

"*Bonjour.*"

Sam's spine almost ripped out of his back when he heard the voice.

"Papa, why are you here?"

"I forgot my suitcase, with all the papers." Clement pointed to the brown leather case on the kitchen table. "And you?" He looked at his daughter with an endearing smile, then glanced over at Sam with polite hostility.

"Oh yes, papa this is Sam," she said and led Sam over to her father. "Sam this is my father."

"*Ashante,*" Sam said in his best French accent. The father was wiry and had a wrinkled, weathered face. And he seemed hard. The sort of stare Sam had seen in the Army.

"*Demem.*" Clement replied.

Adele looked at both and with a devilish grin. "Oh, I forgot something at the neighbors. I'll be right back."

Sam tilted his head at Adele as she walked out the door. She flashed him a playful grin and wondered what she was up to. He looked back at the father and, seeing his hard eyes taking him in, wondered if they would get locked in some sort of stare down. Childish at it sounded, sometimes things boiled down to their simplest element, and this looked like a possible alpha male showdown. But he would have none of that. Sam walked over to the window and looked at the view of a just a busy street. The bustle had a memorized Sam, and he thought of what he had planned on saying to Adele.

"What do you do?" asked Clement.

Sam was jolted out of his daydream. "Me? Right now just traveling. You know taking some time off."

"From what?"

Sam glanced at the open door again, hoping Adele would come through and save him from this interrogation. He looked back at the old man. "Well," he said, his mind deciding how much information to give up.

"How are you two doing?" Adele smiled.

"Just fine." Sam smiled back and turned back to the old man.

Clement had visibly lightened up, but his eyes were still on Sam. "Yes, just fine," he said and walked towards the door and hugged his daughter. "I have to go now. I'm already getting behind on work." He kissed her and walked out.

Adele shut the door behind her and looked at Sam. "He's very protective of me. Especially now that mama is gone."

"He seemed... nice."

"So what was it you were going to tell me?"

Sam remembered what he was going to say and remembered the gravity of it all. Right now he was hoping for a better time to say it. As Adele walked up to him his thoughts focused on her form in front of him. Blood started to rush through his body. "Tell you?"

"Yes," she said and slid her arms around him. "You grabbed me and were going to say something."

He could smell her again, that sweet smell. He had thought it might have been some kind of perfume, but now was sure it was just her sweat. "Oh yeah." His hand slid up to her cheek and traced a line with his finger to her lips. "I forgot."

"Oh?"

He pulled her in close, closed his eyes, and sniffed her neck. "You smell absolutely wonderful."

Adele tilted her head back and closed her eyes.

Sam moved his nose slowly to her lips, and then paused for a second. He moved his head closer. He took in her lower lip and touched it with his tongue. It was a salty, sweet taste that made him want more. He pressed her soft body against his and could feel the heat.

Sam took of his shirt and shifted his hand around her dress. She backed off, undid the back and let it fall to the ground.

Sam was drifting to sleep when he felt a wind on his face. He thought for a second that maybe he was on the beach, the cool ocean wind blowing in. He opened his eyes, and there was her face. It broke into a smile.

"So what does that say?" She pointed at his tattoo a fiery dragon with Old English script twisting around it, shredded with enough scar tissue to be unreadable.

"Nothing, just that it's better to die on your feet than to live on your knees."

Adele traced the words with her finger. "Was this the young idealistic Sam?"

"Yes, the younger naïve one. He's dead."

"You don't believe in these words anymore?"

"No," Sam said then thought about it for a second. He hadn't given those words any thought in a long time. "Not with the same energy as when I got the tattoo."

"That's sad." Adele continued to run her finger over the tattoo. "The words are beautiful."

"Do you want to know what has been on my mind?" he said.

"Something has been bothering you all day," she said and smiled. "It had to wait till after the sex, huh?" She tugged his ear ever so slightly.

"Well something that good should never be kept waiting."

"Of course not." She play-slapped him, and bit her lip.

"No, listen." He moved back to get some space for his words.

"Okay."

"Remember when I said I was just traveling around?" He steeled himself. If she didn't like what it was he was doing, then he was wrong about her. He rolled on to his back so as he could stare at the white ceiling. "Well I lied."

Adele didn't say anything.

"I'm not what you think," Sam continued.

"Then what are you?" She stared intently as Sam went silent again. "If you're not ready I understand."

Sam took a deep breath. Since they'd met it was like they could feel each other's thoughts. "I don't regret anything I ever did in Iraq, not once. There was death everywhere and this wore me down, but I have not a single regret. I'm proud of all I've done." Sam went silent. Was that true? He wasn't sure. He fought back thinking about the kid without the face.

"Of course you should be." Adele looked at him with a furrowed forehead. "What are you really thinking about?"

"What do you mean?"

"Is it that hard for you?"

"I don't know what you mean." Sam's steady gaze started to dart about.

"Yeah you do."

"Stop this shit," Sam said, fidgeting with the bed sheets. Now he wished he hadn't said anything.

"Stop what?"

"Trying to dig into me."

"Why?"

"Because."

"Because of what?"

"Because you're not going to like what you find."

"I'm a grown woman; I can handle it."

"Or so you think."

"I think what? At least I've been honest with you, opened up to you. You're too scared to do the same, or maybe you just don't care."

"Shut up."

"Shut up about what? Do you care?"

Sam didn't answer her. A sinking feeling settled on his heart. He felt her moving away from him.

"Well either you do or you don't." Adele's voice was filled with pain. "At least say something," she said as she moved her face closer to his.

"What are you talking about?"

"You know what I'm talking about."

"This is ridiculous." Sam rolled over and got out of bed. He wasn't sure what he was doing.

"Just tell me if you care or not."

Sam didn't reply as he put on his clothes as quickly as possible.

"Well? What am I? Just some French girl you wanted to fuck?"

Sam shook his head. "I'm getting the outta here. This is crazy." Without so much as glancing at her, he walked out.

CHAPTER 16

"So, you bang that chick yet?" asked Justin.

"Don't worry about it."

"Meaning yes?"

"Yeah."

"Well it's about time man, I was starting to worry about you," Justin said and gave Sam a light punch on the arm.

"But she went psycho on me."

"Those are the best ones. The freaks are always psycho. Besides how do you think you come across? Like you're normal?"

"She tried to start a fight with me today, and I barely know her."

"Wow." Justin whistled.

"That's what I'm saying. Why—"

"No, I mean 'wow' you actually got into an argument. You're usually ditch a chick when that happens." Justin grinned at his friend. "You never get attached to bitches like this."

"The fuck you mean; 'attached'?"

"Oh you definitely like this one eh?"

"What ever."

"You really must like her."

"Fuck you."

"Man that's those are the words of a man in love, don't forget to invite me to the wedding."

"Fuck off..." Sam said. He was angrier than he should have been. "So anything new?"

"No, not at all. In fact I say we start prepping for a hit right away."

"Same habits as the night before?" Sam sat down on a chair.

"Same. I say we hit him at eleven o' clock. That's around when the last customers leave. So we can hang around a little longer than normal."

"Not together," Sam said.

"Yeah, one at the bar, the other at a table. There's a restroom upstairs. One will go up, the other will follow after a text, or set time."

Sam nodded his head. He was glad they would get on with this and be done with it. He had come to an agreement with himself that this would be the last hit he would do. He had yet to discuss this with Justin. He felt guilty about it but figured it would wait until after the hit. No need to complicate things right now. They had a mission to do. "Good deal, what about his gorilla?"

"Not there at night. He probably stays elsewhere."

"Method?"

"Yeah, I'm doing it."

"Of course." Sam waved his hand.

"Knife, but with a handgun as backup. I figure the quieter the better."

"All right."

"That's about all I have for now. I figure we can go through it a few times."

"Yeah, and all the alternate plans," Sam said and looked out through the window. "You remember how it looked right?"

"Yeah, to a 'T'. I got the steps counted out and everything."

"Nice." Sam thought through everything they would have to go over. "We'll go over a few plans this afternoon."

"Yeah, let me get some sleep first and we'll rock it."

"Good deal." Sam was happy now. The thought of the hit reminded him of what he enjoyed doing. He could feel that adrenaline rush, and he smiled. He looked at his friend. They had been through so much together. He remembered a time they'd chatted in Iraq.

"This sucks."

"Yeah it does." Justin double checked his SAW and lay it down on the sandbags. Their squad had been stuck with guard duty for the week, and it was wearing thin on everyone. The hours weren't too bad, eight a day, but it was tedious and uneventful. Luckily, Justin and Sam had managed to be together so they talked away the time. Now, though, they had run out of subjects to talk about.

"Why the fuck are we out here anyways? Isn't there a fucking insurgency to put down?" Sam yelled out.

"I don't know man. I think they're giving us a break."

"We don't need a fucking break. Everyday we stand out here we get weaker. And everyday haj squats in the gutter, he gets stronger."

Justin chuckled. "All right Captain Willard, don't go over the edge on me just yet."

Sam made a sucking sound with the side of his mouth to show his disgust. "What the fuck ever man."

Justin shook his head. "You're a piece of work."

"I know, but that's what makes me so awesome."

"Did I forget modest?"

"Fuuck you."

They stood in silence. In the distance flickered the lights of a village. They were wrapped in as many layers of clothing as they could scavenge. It was winter in Iraq, and out here in the desert with the whipping wind, it was cold. Standing still for hours on end didn't help.

"This is way too fucking cold for my tastes man." Sam stomped his feet. It hadn't been an hour, and he was already losing the feeling to his toes. "I hope we get attacked, at least we'll warm up then."

"Yeah, that would be great. Nut."

"Christ knows I'm tired of talking to your ass." Sam grinned at his friend.

"What do you think? I like talking to you? Hearing your bohemian tragedy of a life story?"

Sam burst out laughing. "Screw you prick and your meth riddled hillbilly saga."

They both laughed, trying to keep it as muffled as possible.

"Naw man, I'm glad we're on the same team."

"Yeah." Sam wiped the smile off his face. "Me too man. I think we're both crazy enough to make it outta here alive."

"*Inshallah.*"

"Exactly. *Inshallah.*"

They huddled closer together for warmth as the wind picked up again.

"You know what? When I die I really don't care what happens to my body."

Sam gave his friend a raised eyebrow. "Well that's random."

"But you know what I'm saying? People are always making a big deal about that shit. I'll be fucking dead. Why the fuck should I care what happens to my body?"

"I guess." Sam maintained his goofy face to emphasize how odd the statement was.

"I mean either way it's getting absorbed by the earth, right?"

"I'd imagine it's mainly for your family."

"I still don't care."

"Yeah I gotcha," Sam said forcefully, not liking the subject. "I suppose I don't care either to what happens to my body... you could piss on it for all I care."

Sam woke up. He looked out the window, it was evening but it wasn't too late. He nudged Justin. "Wake up."

Justin rolled over. "Huh."

"We need to go over some plans."

"I know, I know." Justin planted his face in the pillow then pushed himself off the bed.

Sam walked into the bathroom and rinsed his face out. When he came back into the room Justin was sitting up. Sam pulled out a chair and sat down next to Justin. "Well let's make a model first."

"Okay," Justin got up and rummaged through his suitcase. He grabbed some yarn and little plastic army figures. He then proceeded to make a floor plan of the restaurant on the floor. He paused to look at Sam. "Don't forget the door."

"Oh yeah." Sam walked to the door. He put on the 'do not disturb' sign, then locked and chained up the door, before he sat back down.

When Justin was finished he looked up. "This look right?"

Sam nodded his head. "Okay, so the hit goes down inside the restaurant."

"Uh huh. Outside only if he somehow slips out, but we need to do everything to prevent that from happening."

"Right, so we hit him upstairs."

"Was there a window in that alleyway?" asked Justin.

Sam tried to think back. "Yeah, it's probably to his room, but that shouldn't be an issue."

"I'd imagine not. We'll be coming up the stairs, so that eliminates that as an escape route for him. This should all be a surprise to him, so he won't be so far away we can't shoot him."

"Plus a second story fall; he'll stumble a little if he doesn't break something."

"Giving us a little time."

"We still want to avoid any shooting outside," Sam said again.

"Of course."

"Now for the timing," Sam said and duly wrote down their analysis. "You were saying?"

"Around eleven to eleven thirty at night the place closes down."

"No exact time?"

"Nope."

"So we'll have to be ready at eleven, adjusting as needed."

"Well," Sam said and rubbed his chin. "Make it before eleven. To be inside when we do the hit, so might as well do it when the place is still open. Don't have to break in."

"Okay, but how do we do it? We can't just walk in there and walk upstairs. We don't need our faces to be seen."

"We'll use ski masks," Justin said and pointed to their suitcase full of clothes.

"Naw." Sam shook his head. "It'll attract too much attention."

"What then?"

"You know what?" Sam snapped his fingers. "In the kitchen there was a fuse box."

"You sure?"

"I'll go through the back. If Didier is working I'll just tie him up, hit the fuse box and lights out will be your cue to come in."

"You have zip strips?"

"Yeah, I got 'em."

"Okay, I'll come through the front door, that way there's less risk of ol' Pyotr slipping out." Justin lifted up an army figure to indicate which one represented Pyotr.

"Good, now if we can do this without using our flashlights, downstairs at least, we'll be golden. Everyone will be confused."

"Well, I remember the exact steps and the layout, so I'll be fine. What about you?"

"The fuse box was right next to the bar door, so I should be able to manage that."

"Well, if all's that bad you can use your flashlight."

"Okay, but I'll try not to."

"All right, so we're going upstairs." Justin paused to move two figures up the make shift stairs.

"First we need a recognition symbol for when we meet at the stairs. It's gonna be pretty dark."

"Uhh, what about eagle's nest?" Justin said.

"No, that would give us away as American's. We need it in French so the witnesses have less to give to the cops." Sam looked at the nightstand to think of something French. "How about *bon voyage?*"

"You say *voyage* the counter is *bon?*"

"Yup."

"Sounds good. So we walk up the stairs." Justin moved the figures again.

"How many?"

"Twelve, the rail ends on the last step so it'll be a sufficient guide."

Sam wrote some more notes down. "All right, so now we're upstairs."

"Of course, ol' Pyotr sees the lights go out he won't think much of it. He hears boots running up his stairs right after that and he's going to figure it out pretty easily."

"Yeah, so quiet until we get to the door."

"The door was locked when I checked it out, but it felt flimsy. One donkey kick should take it down."

"Good, so we turn our flashlights on and go in."

"Right, so here we're at a loss because we don't know the layout of his little apartment."

They both paused to picture the problem in their minds and how to deal with it.

"That's gonna suck, but it's not gonna be some maze. We can work with it," Sam said.

"Exactly. If we catch him with his pants down I can just execute him with a knife."

"Uh huh," Sam said and mentally flinched. Now that they were close to the killing the knife method sounded barbaric.

"Otherwise we shoot."

"Shooting means we get the fuck outta dodge as quickly as possible. But with the knife choice we can leave without rushing, just make sure you don't get too much blood on your clothes."

"Oh don't worry about that. I'll slice his throat facing away from us."

"Okay. Also I think we should exit through that window."

"Jump out of it?"

"That way if the lights have come on, our faces won't be seen. Easier to get out that way."

Justin looked at the floor plan. "In that case when coming through the kitchen make sure that door is locked and secured somehow."

"Will do. Also make sure the alley is clear for a jump."

"Right. Now on to the alternate plans."

Once again they both paused in silence to let their minds picture the situation. Allowing their experience to come up with reactions to those scenarios.

"I really can't think of anything. I suppose we could use some Molotov-cocktails as a distraction downstairs," Sam said and rested his head on his hands.

"But that's gonna bring way too many eyes our way."

"Plus the police might come earlier. Remember people are quick to call in fires more than anything else. We should still have it as a distraction. In case we get into a prolonged firefight or in case Pyotr gets holed in and our handguns aren't enough to flush him out. Then we'll use it."

"Also in case we have company during our exit."

"I get it, we can use it as a distraction and obstacle when we're leaving. People will move to the fire as we get outta there." Sam moved the figures to mimmick the escape plan.

"You still remember how to make that firebomb mix?"

"Yeah, we'll need to hit up a gas station and general store for the ingredients."

"And leave that shit in the car," Justin said and pointed at Sam.

"We'll mix it a few hours before the hit and leave it in the car. Besides tonight should be our last night here in the hotel. Then it's our car as base camp from then on."

91

"Remove it from the garage?"

"The day of, yeah, park it somewhere nearby. Make sure it's not in someplace illegal."

"I know the perfect place. About a ten minute walk from the restaurant."

"Sounds good." Sam leaned back on his chair. His mind was wound tight just thinking about the plan. "Pass me a smoke man."

Justin lit one, threw it at Sam, then lit his own.

"You know what we need?" Sam asked not really waiting for an answer. "We need cocaine for these sessions."

"Yeah." Justin chuckled. "You're telling me."

"Well you're pretty much boys with Pyotr. Why don't you hook it up?"

"Sure fucking thing, asshole," Justin laughed.

Sam sucked in a nicotine hit, relaxing his mind. The tobacco burning smelled familiar and he closed his eyes.

"What about if he has company up there?"

"All we can do is speed surprise then violence of action. That should take care of all contingencies, that I can think of at least."

"I mean like a woman or something, like in Spain."

"Well we'll be careful. Our usual rules, we don't hurt innocents."

"Okay."

There was a pause as they thought of all the possible scenarios.

"Another method for taking out the lights?" Justin released a plume of smoke as he spoke.

"We could take out a junction box nearby. But I'm not feeling that route. We'd have to recon just to make sure it was the right box for the restaurant. We're just two men. The fuse box doesn't work and now I'm going to set up the junction box? Even if we work inwards, junction box first then fuse box. We do the j-box how? It'll be out in the open. People will see us. We don't have uniforms or anything to look like electricians working on it."

"Okay," Justin muttered. "So that's out the window."

"I figure the fuse box doesn't work we'll go to ski masks."

"Okay, I'm waiting outside for the lights to go out. If that doesn't happen I'm waiting for a text?"

"I guess, can you think of anything else?"

"No, but if I hear nothing for a minute I'll walk in anyways."

"Good, also we gotta try texting around there before we part ways, just to make sure it works."

"Yeah, no blackout spots."

"Right and if it's a text you don the ski mask."

"Then we meet at the stairs."

"But first if the lights are on I'll tell everyone to get down."

"You handle that, you know *le* French," Justin used his best French accent and waved his cigarette vigorously.

Sam took his friend's jab in stride.

"I don't think we need to yell anything downstairs for the lights on situation."

"No?" Sam said and reached for another cigarette.

"No, people are fucking sheep. They'll probably stare in shock. Should anyone move we pistol whip them and it will keep the rest in line."

"Fair enough. Now for the escape plan."

Justin shrugged his shoulders. "Jump out that window, right?"

"But after that we tuck our weapons and walk away."

"Separate after the alleyway."

"All right."

"I want us to use baby wipes to wipe excess blood and have a spare set of clothes so we can change on the move, or in some dark alley."

Sam smiled. "Roger that gunny."

"Can you think of anything else, prick?"

"No, I think we're good."

"Then let's walk through it a few times."

The two of them made a few adjustments to their room and started going through the motions.

When they had gone through movements enough to be sufficiently satisfied with their plan, Sam decided they had enough. "Let's take a break and go do this in some bigger area," he said.

"Where?" asked Justin.

"I know a spot, it's perfect."

The two gathered their things and went out to practice the hit. For more than two hours they went through their plan.

They got back to the hotel around nine at night. Both were feeling pretty exhausted from the repetitious day.

"I'm gonna head out man."

"Okay." Justin gave his friend an odd look. "The French chick?"

"Yeah, I just need to say something to her."

"What? I thought she was a psycho?"

"Maybe, but who isn't?"

"Sure man, just don't fall in love before we have to do this mission."

"I know what's up. Don't worry."

CHAPTER 17

Sam met up with Adele at *Le Port*.

"So what is it?" Adele still had anger lingering in her voice.

"Nothing," Sam said.

"Nothing?"

"Just listen for a second." Sam grabbed her by her belt loop and pulled her closer to him. He looked in her eyes then let go.

"What is it?"

Sam laughed. "Shhh listen."

"Stop playing these games."

"Come on." Sam took her hand and they started walking. "I love this place at night."

Adele didn't say anything.

"The lights of the buildings, the dark sea, the quiet rocking of the boats, the background lull of the street. I love it."

Adele stayed silent.

"You ever wonder where life will take you?" Sam waited for an answer then looked over at Adele.

Adele looked back at him. "Always."

"Does it ever scare you?"

"Sometimes, but sometimes you feel like you can face anything."

"So which are you feeling right now?"

"I don't know."

"You're not scared are you?"

"Not like before."

"What scared you before?" Sam sat them down on the edge of the port.

"You know how I was part of *Medicins Sans Frontieres*? Well after a while I got sick of everything and went off on my own."

"On your own?"

"Yes, me and some friends, working with local doctors. We were in Congo and our camp got overrun by rebels in the middle of the night... I hid under my bed, and they walked around in my hut. I could see their feet and the barrels of their Kalashnikovs." Adele held on to Sam. "All I could think of at that moment was I didn't want to die, and I wanted to see my parents. I hadn't seen them in so long... They killed my friend... A local doctor called Chipago. I left the next day. I went to Nairobi, that's when I got the message that my mother was close to death. So I came back." Adele was barely whispering as she relived the moment staring off into the dark sea. "She was already dead. Since then I've been scared of life... confused." Adele looked at Sam. "Until I met you. I'm still confused, but you've been perfect, and yet I still think you're holding something back. For some reason you're still scared to tell me."

"I know." Sam took out the tiny carved dragon he had in his pocket and placed it in her hand.

"What's this?" She looked at it and rolled it around in her palm.

"Just something I found."

Adele looked at it for a moment, twirling it around in her fingers before putting it away in her pocket. "So what are you really doing here?"

He looked down at her. "You really want to know?"

"Of course, I wouldn't ask would I?"

"It's not pretty."

"I'm a grown woman Sam. I can handle it. What I can't handle you lying to me."

"Okay," he said. "Ever since I left the Army I've been traveling around Europe with my friend. We've been robbing people for money. Mostly drug dealers... we've even killed a few." Sam could feel Adele's stare, but he didn't bother looking at her. Right now that dark body of sea was all he wanted to take in. "I didn't like it... but I didn't hate it either." Sam looked around at *Le Port*. "A few months ago, right here, something bad happened. My friend's sister stole something very important from someone very dangerous. She was killed for that... that insolence... that's why I'm here, I'm helping him get revenge. I don't know much Adele. I know I'm not proud of what I've done. I know I want to change, and I know, more than anything else, I have to help my friend."

"That's it?" she said.

"Yeah," Sam smiled. "That's it."

They sat without speaking for a while until Adele broke the silence with a barrage of questions. They were mostly inquisitive, small details which Sam couldn't see any reason for knowing but complied anyways.

"I've gotta go Adele."

"Already?"

"Yes."

"Okay. We'll talk again won't we?"

"Of course Adele."

They parted ways.

Adele walked into her room and flopped down. Things had changed so suddenly. Sam was definitely a little darker now that she knew this about him. Yet she still had the same feelings for him.

She heard her father walk in. He was back early again. He walked into her room.

"Hello papa."

"Hi Adele, what's wrong?"

Adele sat up and looked at her father. They had always been so close. She had always confided in him as she grew up, told him her dreams, everything. But when she came back she had been silent. She had changed so much, seen so much, she thought there was no way he could ever understand. She was no longer his little girl. She was certain he hadn't forgiven her for not being around when her mother needed her the most. But now she was lost again. She didn't know what to do and looking at her father brought back that feeling again. The feeling that she was young and all she had to do was tell him her problems and they would vanish away into thin air.

Adele's father sat down next to her. "Come on Adele, you can tell me. I'm old, but I'm still your father."

"Oh papa," she said and sniffled. A tear trickled slowly and turned into stream as she shook in her father's arms. "I'm so lost right now."

"Why Adele?"

"I met a man. He's great...But... I just don't know."

Clement smiled wistfully and remained quiet.

"I've never felt this strongly about a man before, and now he might not be what I first thought." She wasn't going to tell him everything since she didn't want to break Sam's trust.

"What do you mean Adele?" Clement spread his arm around her shoulders.

"He used to be a soldier, American. He got out, but I think he has certain habits he hasn't lost."

"Adele, this man... He obviously has been through a lot. War tends to do a lot of things to men." He stood up and walked up to the nightstand where a framed photo of the family at the beach stood.

Adele nodded as her father picked up the picture and sat down next to her.

"I remember how beautiful you were, and all the boys were trying to chase you that summer." He smiled.

"Yes," Adele said. "I remember mama had to tell you to stop staring down all the boys."

"Yes, I know. A father tends to be protective. Your mother, she was great. You know from the moment I set my eyes on her, I knew we were going to be together for the rest of our lives. This man, Sam." He paused and handed the photo to her. "Only you know what you feel for him." He looked at his daughter. "You understand?"

"Yes," Adele said and shifted. This wasn't the father she remembered.

Clement shuffled his feet uncomfortably before excusing himself.

CHAPTER 18

That morning Sam and Justin packed all their things they would need for the hit. They made sure their backpacks had extra ammo, baby wipes, and a change of clothes. They checked out of their hotel room and parked the car in a place they were certain wouldn't attract attention. They went to eat some breakfast and go over the adjustments they'd made. That's when Sam's phone started to ring. It was Adele. He ignored it at first, but after the fifth call he answered. He talked for a few seconds in what appeared to be grunts then hung up.

"I gotta go man," Sam said.

"Christ man, she loves the dick that much?" Justin's voice had a hint of anger.

"I guess."

"You must have really given it to her."

"Hey it's something I was born with," Sam said and grinned. "I'll be back in a couple hours, okay?" Sam gave Justin a pleading look. He didn't want to leave his friend if there were any doubts between them.

"All right man, make it a quickie. I'll be waiting in the car."

Adele wasn't one to feel uncertain about anything. And though Sam had thrown her a curve ball that previous night, she was now more certain than ever. She saw Sam and they embraced. The smell of his deodorant and the strength in his arms made her feel safe.

"So?" Sam looked at her.

"So, I've decided," she said and took him by the arm as they walked down the promenade. "That I don't want any part of a hit man."

"I told you... this isn't for me."

"Promise?"

"Yeah, I promise."

"Okay." Adele felt a warm feeling in her body. She felt extremely connected to every breath Sam took. They walked in silence down the promenade.

"Where do you wanna go after this?"

"Go?" Adele gave Sam a curious look. "I like the Mediterranean."

"I'm not staying here after tonight."

"I don't know," she said. "Where ever you want to go."

"When I was a kid I had this picture of an island. The sea was blue, like an angel's eyes and there were white washed buildings. I kept that picture with me until it wore out. It inspired me then. At the worst of times when I felt like there was no hope I'd look at it and it would bring me back to life. It was as if I believed I was there." Sam looked at Adele. "At the time it saved me from the death of hope. But it's been a long time since I've hoped." He looked off to the sea then back at her. "I think I know that there's something to live for."

They walked in silence again. A group of French teenagers laughed underneath some palm trees. She held Sam's hand and felt truly at peace.

"I know the perfect place." Adele said. "It's an island off Greece. It's just as you described the picture. It's heaven on earth."

"Really?"

"Yes really. I was there when I was a kid."

"Then that's where we'll go."

"What will you do?"

"I'll be doing you," Sam said and grinned.

"Asshole," she said and punched him on the shoulder. "Besides that."

"Oh? What else is there?" Sam glanced at Adele with a grin.

"Shut up." She laughed. "I mean for money."

"Oh that. I don't know. Maybe set up a bar, or ferry couples to romantic spots on the islands."

"Or both."

"That sounds about right, but we have forever to decide that."

They went back to her place for one more taste of each other. Afterwards, they lay on top of each other, a layer of sweat between them, and traded promises.

As Adele watched Sam leave she blurted out her request: "Promise me you'll be back."

Sam stopped and walked back over to Adele. "You know what Adele?"

"What?"

"All my life I felt like I've had to run... just running away from... I don't know, everything. It always felt forced—a need more than a want," he said and looked into her eyes. "I maybe running away again, but this time it feels right. Because you're going to be there by my side." He held her arms and pulled her closer. "I promise baby. I'll be back." Sam kissed her.

"Nice of you to show up." Justin made an obvious glance at his watch.

"My bad man."

"Fuck Sam. Is this anytime to be chasing some pussy? You know how important this is, right?"

"I said I messed up okay?"

Justin stared at Sam for a second before finally looking away.

They double checked all their equipment and weapons and went to grab a final bite to eat. After they returned to the car they took a power nap.

Half an hour before hit time, they woke up and walked to their objective. They milled about the narrow alleyways of *Vieux* Nice without saying a word. Each was getting into the right mind frame. About a block from the restaurant they checked to make sure they could text each other. They re-synchronized their watches and without a word parted ways.

CHAPTER 19

Sam walked towards the restaurant, his nervousness slowly fading. It was always like this, he would get apprehensive and doubt his abilities, but as the moment approached his mind grew clearer, and he felt untouchable.

From the alley, Sam could see Didier whistling and washing some utensils in the kitchen. Sam sneaked in and hid behind the oven.

Sam fingered the handgrip of the handgun he'd tucked in his pants. He didn't want to kill Didier, but he would knock him out if needed.

Sam took out his ski mask, put it on, took a deep breath, and moved a few feet behind Didier. Sam crouched and waited for a second before he leapt behind Didier and jammed the handgun into his back.

"*Haut les mains*," Sam said.

Didier's shaking hands went up.

"*Baissez-vous.*"

Didier, still trembling, lay down.

"*Ne bouge pas, piger?!*"

"*Oui.*"

Sam took out his zip strips and cinched Didier's hands and feet together. Sam walked up to the fuse box and turned off everything.

Sam moved into the restaurant. He could hear a few customers laughing about the dark situation. When he bumped into a man he gave the password: "*Bon.*"

"*Voyage.*"

They moved up the stairs.

Sam twisted the knob ever so slightly. He felt it give, and he leaned on it with his shoulder and pushed it open.

Sam took a couple of steps in and stopped. Justin closed the door and came up beside Sam and gave him a squeeze. They turned on their flashlights and moved forward.

There was an open room a few feet to their left, and the hallway opened up into a room in the back. The hallway was narrow so Justin stayed behind Sam.

The man came out in a flash. Sam protected his weapon with his non-firing hand. Sam's head snapped back as the man threw a punch. It stung; he could taste salty blood in his mouth. He cocked his right hand back and fired a shot at the man. Sam saw the pain in the man's face. The man seemed too big to care about a mere nine millimeters of projectile going through him. And he lunged forward again.

From behind, Justin flew at the man. The force and placement of it was enough to stop the man in his tracks and push him back. The man reached to grab Justin. Justin's right hand came forward with his weapon and as soon as his barrel touched the man's neck his barrel flashed.

Aleksei was exhausted. He and Pyotr had been working for the better part of the night on another plan for more cocaine shipments. They'd decided to keep all their options open and continue with drug mules on commercial planes and boats in addition to the major shipments on private boats. The Haitians had turned out to be a godsend and it was just a matter of not to get caught.

He went to the dining room for a bite to eat. Pyotr was still in his room writing out some details on how they were going to get in all the shipments. The lights went out and Aleksei didn't think much of it. He fumbled for a flashlight. That's when he heard the door open. His skin prickled, and he felt the hairs on his back stand. He'd left his weapon in the other room. Aleksei heard the door shut. Pyotr had been talking about the possibility of someone coming after him. This was it.

Aleksei had always been one for action and crouched next to the door. He could see the flashlights moving closer. As soon as he saw the barrel of the gun, he leapt left hand reaching out. The handgun moved away from his hands. But Aleksei's right elbow was cocked and cracked into the man's jaw. He felt the man's head whip back. It gained Aleksei a valuable second as he reached to grab the smaller man. Then he heard the shot go off and knew that his effort wouldn't be enough—the great equalizer had spoken. The smaller man knew what he was doing and had shielded his weapon from Aleksei with his body. The bullet went right through Aleksei's chest, knocking him back, but not over. Aleksei lunged again for the smaller man. He could feel the heat in his chest growing.

That's when Aleksei caught the blow to his neck. Aleksei tried to grab the bigger man. He still stood a chance if he could make this a pure hand-to-hand fight.

But it was too quick to stop. Before Aleksei's nerve endings could even sense the cold steel in contact with his neck the cold had already changed to heat. Hot flash, hot bullet as it traveled up through his throat. Brain, flesh, and other assorted liquids sprayed the wall and ceiling. Aleksei collapsed. His valiant effort against greater odds had come to an end.

Pyotr heard the noise of a fight. He got up and heard the gunshot. He didn't hesitate. He leapt from his window into the alley below and heard the second gunshot. As he sprinted through the alleyways he knew he was going to have to figure out how to get whoever did this. It wouldn't be easy. First he had to get out of town. He had to get out of here and regroup with those that he trusted the most.

Eric was walking down the alleyway of *Vieux* Nice, exasperated at being lost. In his hand was a British chick he'd picked up at the bar. She was too drunk to know where she was either. But he had a room for that night and wasn't about to waste the money. His Europe trip so far had been great. Every city he'd gone through he'd caught some thing warm to sleep with. Tonight shouldn't be any different. He looked down an alley; it seemed to be a dead end. That's when he heard the gunshot and saw the flash from the window. Then a second gunshot was met with a man jumping out of the window and falling onto the alleyway. He bounced off the ground and in one smooth motion came running at them. He sprinted by them and disappeared down another alley.

Eric had seen a lot of emotions in his life. The fear on this man's face was distinctly one of survival. Two men more jumped out the window. One right after the other each landed and looked both ways before running. He could see the steel in each of their hands. Eric stepped back. One ran by him and didn't so much as look at him. The other was a few feet behind, but Eric noticed him staring right at him. Cold eyes. Eric raised his hand to show he was no threat. The man ran at him then lowered his shoulder and hit him right in the chest. Eric went flying back and hit a wall.

The man seemed to have used him as something to bounce off and kept running after his friend. Eric was a restive college kid and would have fought over this, but he'd seen the gun and knew better. As his British girl helped him up he shifted his mind back to his original thoughts. After all, this wasn't his fight. Obviously someone was going to be that guy that died tonight. Eric would just have to be that guy that got laid.

Sam ran after Justin. His legs moved faster than he ever thought possible. He knew his friend's emotions were running high right now. But the last thing they needed to do was get arrested for not acting rationally. Right now the rational thing to do was not run around Nice after two gunshots had been fired. Running with guns drawn was beyond irrational. It was stupid. Sam tucked his gun in his pants as he closed the distance to Justin.

Sam grabbed Justin by the shoulder. "Justin, stop!" He stood in front of his friend and sucked in air. "Put the gun away."

Justin looked at his friend menacingly, then complied.

"We can't get caught man," Sam said in a lowered voice. "This place is going to be crawling with cops soon enough. We need to play it smart and get outta here, right now." Sam took out his bandanna and wiped some of Aleksei's head off Justin's face. "We'll get him. I fucking promise you that, but we gotta lay low for now."

Justin nodded his head, he seemed to be in a daze. "Where do we go? How do we find him again?"

"Don't worry man. We'll get him."

CHAPTER 20

Adele heard the knock on her door, and her heart jumped. She'd been reading some information about the island in Greece. She opened the door and saw Sam. Next to him was another man, his face covered in blood. Her heart stopped. But Sam was here. She ushered them in.

She dabbed Sam's face with a handkerchief. His lip was swollen, and he had some blood in his mouth. Sam's friend merely nodded his head at her before going off to wash himself. She walked to the kitchen and poured some water for all of them. Someone had been killed. She was going to ask Sam, but from the looks on their faces she decided not to.

Justin walked out of the bathroom and after wiping his face with the towel looked at both of them. He raised his eyebrows, gave a questioning look, and pointed at his face. Sam nodded his head and gave a thumbs up.

"Okay, we'll get some sleep now," said Adele as she showed Justin his place on the couch. A white sheet and pillow were laid out for him. Adele gave him a glass of water. "Good night," she smiled briefly.

Adele walked over to Sam. Sam nodded at Justin, took Adele by the hand and they walked into her room.

Sam woke up, his dream jolting him out of his sleep. He glanced at his watch, six o'clock. Not too late, though he'd hoped to wake up earlier. Adele murmured in her sleep. He smiled as her face crunched, and she murmured again. Her face yesterday had been forgiving. She'd been quiet and understood they needed silence. He knew he would have to explain what had happened to this woman who had, for a brief moment in his dark life, brought in some light, made him stop and think about what he was doing. Now he felt that was about to slip away. He had a job to do. Justin needed him. It was as simple as that.

Adele woke up and looked at him. Her smile melted into a frown. She waited expectedly.

"What is it?" Adele squinted her eyes at Sam.

Sam just nodded his head, not at her question but to some distant thought.

"So, what happened? Just tell me the truth."

"All right, you really wanna know?" He paused. "Well we tried the hit, but the guy's bodyguard was there. By the time we killed him... the main guy escaped."

"The crime boss?"

"Yes, he got away."

"So what now?"

"We have to go after him... finish him off."

Adele paused to take that in. "How?" she asked, "It can't be easy."

"I never said it would."

"What do you mean? He's a powerful man, how do you know he's not hunting you right now?"

"I don't, but that's why I have to hit him before he hits me."

"Just the two of you? That's crazy... that's suicide."

"You don't understand."

"Don't understand what?"

"I'm going to get him."

"How can you be certain?"

"We're going to get him."

Adele's face shrunk back. "Will you live through it?"

Sam didn't answer.

"Sam? Will you?" She started to breath fast. "Answer me Sam."

"That doesn't matter. What matters is we have to kill him. I owe that much to Justin."

"And what about us? Weren't we supposed to go to Greece?"

"What do you want me to do?"

"Come to Greece with me," she pleaded.

Sam sighed. He felt his heart crumple. "You know I can't."

"I know... Please don't die."

Sam kissed her on her forehead. "Of course not."

Justin woke up to hear voices coming from the kitchen. They were whispers, barely under a scream. He recognized Sam's voice, and the voice of the woman from last night. He liked her addictive French accent. As he heard them fighting, he could tell through her strained voice that it was against her very nature to be like this. He imagined neither Sam nor Adele were used to fighting like this. Justin rubbed the grime out of his eyes.

"You want some breakfast man?" Sam had a plate of omelet in each hand. Behind him Adele walked out. Whatever strain she'd in her voice, wasn't on her face. As Sam put the plates down, she looked over at Justin and smiled.

Justin rubbed his eyes again, pretending that he was doing it for the first time. "Yeah, man it sounds just about right." He threw off the bed sheet and walked up to the table. Sam and Adele sat across from each other and Justin sat in the middle. He felt like a child with two parents in the middle of a fight. He grinned.

He could tell that the fight was over the mission. He wasn't surprised that Sam had told Adele what had gone down. She would have wanted an explanation for their messy appearance. Justin looked up at his friend still grinning.

Sam smiled back at him curiously.

"So may I ask what this lover's quarrel is about?" Justin asked.

"Oh it was nothing, just..." Adele looked at Sam.

"I'm Justin by the way," Justin said and offered her his hand, "I don't remember your name, I'm horrible with 'em."

"Adele," she shook his hand and gave a smile.

"He's a motherfucker huh?" Justin was still grinning at Adele.

Adele smiled and nodded her head. "Yes he is."

Sam looked up and shrugged his shoulders in an admission of guilt. He looked down at his empty plate, then over at Justin's plate, still with half an omelet on it. It was the first time he could remember that he'd finished before Justin. He looked over at Justin as if to transfer his urgency to his friend. Silence once again covered the table. Justin caught the glare and finished his omelet.

Soon they were off. Justin walked out the door. Sam paused behind him and looked over at Adele. She was holding the door open for him, but her eyes were on the ground.

"I'm sorry," Sam whispered.

"I know," Adele replied.

She looked up at Sam, with those brown eyes. The ones he took so much comfort in.

"Will..." she said, "you be back?"

Sam felt like breaking down. He could see she felt the same. He took her by the waist and kissed her. If only to taste her, to feel her soft body press against his, to smell her. He pulled away. "I don't know." He took a deep breath, and before he could break down any further, he walked out.

Justin was waiting for Sam outside in the alley. "Nice girl. Now I see why you were late."

"Yeah I know," said Sam. By now he'd gathered most of his emotions together.

"'Yeah I know'? Man, she's awesome, I'd definitely bang her out," Justin said with a grin and gave a louder than warranted chuckle.

The two walked in silence. They sat at a deserted cafe talking about what to do next.

When they'd written down everything they needed to do, Sam went to a pay phone to give Maxime a call. No answer. Maxime's normal message wasn't there anymore, but rather some French lady came on. He didn't know what she said, but he was sure that it meant that Maxime's phone couldn't be located; he could have lost it, but he also could be rolled up. They had to assume the latter. Which meant they were working against the clock.

Sam remembered Didier, the cook. The bar where Sam saw him was a cafe during the day. There was a chance that Didier would show up there. Sam decided he could risk it. Justin hung back while Sam took off.

Sam walked down to the cafe. He glanced inside and saw Didier sitting down to a cup of coffee and a croissant. Sam walked into Didier's field of vision, as nonchalantly as possible, then turned to face him. "Didier?"

"Ahh, Densm. So good to see you."

Sam gave an upwards nod of his head, trying his best to be casual. He was glad Didier remembered him. Sam sat down at the table across from Didier. The waitress came over and Sam ordered a coffee. "Glad to see you've cheered up. You were looking pretty bad before."

"Oh, sometimes things just work out for the best, the best." When the waitress brought over Sam's coffee, Didier raised his cup and their cups clanged in an otherwise silent toast.

"May I ask why?" Sam asked.

"Remember the boss I was telling you about?"

"Oh yeah," Sam said, making an extra effort to seem like he was recalling the information. "You said he was in the mafia or something, right?"

"Well that bastard got what was coming to him," Didier whispered, leaning in.

"What do you mean?" Sam leaned in as well.

"Well, don't tell anyone," Didier said and looked back and forth. "But last night someone tried to kill the bastard."

"No?! That's horrible, why?" Sam forced his hand to his mouth, trying his hardest not to smile.

"No." Didier shook his finger. "The only horrible thing is that they didn't succeed. They only got his fat friend."

"Still... why?" Sam asked.

"The police think it's some inner mob rivalry, but who cares," Didier said and shrugged. "He deserved it. Now I hope they get him."

"No, you mustn't wish death on anyone."

Didier waved off the statement. "Ahh, you don't understand... this man deserves it."

"Ohh," Sam said hesitatingly. "So did he go to the police. You know, so they can help him?"

Didier gave a condescending laugh. "My friend, this man can't go to the police. His entire life has been spent as a criminal, staying away from cops. He's run off to his hideaway in Corse."

Sam's perked up. "Corsica? I've heard it's beautiful there."

"Yes, very."

"Where did he go?"

"I think he has a place near Bastia, but I don't know where exactly."

"Well I hope all's well with him. You can never wish death on anyone."

"I know, still..." Didier replied noncommittally.

Sam poked with a few more questions trying to find if Didier knew anything else. Didier mentioned a distance north from Bastia, a small village name and the fact that the house was the only one for miles. Sam then steered the conversation to a lighter subject and when he felt there was a long enough pause in the dying conversation, he excused himself.

Sam walked out of the cafe as fast as possible. Now they had to head to Corsica, but quickly. Time wasn't a luxury they had. It would take a few days of looking around to find anything. Even then it would be tough. A small town? That was one strike against them. A small town meant that the people in it would get suspicious if Sam and Justin went around asking questions. On the other hand, it was still the height of the tourist season; a couple of Americans looking at the sights wouldn't be much of a problem. They'd have to be careful though, Sam had no idea how well situated Pyotr was in this town. Were the people there wary of him, like Didier was, or were they faithful to him? Being that Pyotr almost had his life taken, he would most likely have paid off a few people to be on the look out for people acting suspiciously or asking too many questions.

When Sam found Justin, they sat down at another cafe and went over all the information. They poured over the map Sam had bought from a bookstore. They made an educated guess with the distance Didier had given them, then made concentric circles around it, marking all the populated areas. They would start the search from the inside going out. Giving extra attention to the populated areas.

After a few hours they put together a plan. They knew they would have to hit the ground in Corsica, being careful not to arouse any suspicion and get more intelligence. Time could not be wasted over-thinking and over-planning.

They walked towards *Le Port*, to buy a ferry ticket out there. It would be risky, but Justin convinced Sam that they didn't have a choice. As they walked down to the kiosk to buy the tickets for the ferry, Sam stopped and tugged on Justin's arm, stopping him as well. "You know what I just thought of?"

"What?"

Adele had spent the entire day sitting around her room wondering how things could have gone bad so quickly. A few days ago she was full of joy, but then everything came to an end this morning. Her emotions, raging all day long, were slowly maturing into something more bearable. She had gone from helpless to hateful. She was angry with herself, but mainly she was angry at Sam for being who he was.

"What is it Adele?" asked Clement when he walked back in.

"Nothing papa."

"Come on now, your eyes have been dried of all their tears. Surely it's something."

"Sam, he..."

"Sam what Adele?"

"He left, and I don't know if he's coming back."

"Why Adele?" Clement waited for an answer, none came. "Come on Adele."

"I don't know what to do papa."

"Well I can't help if you won't tell me anything, can I? Well Adele... if he truly cares about you he'll come back."

Adele walked into the kitchen to grab something to eat. She hadn't had a single bite of food the entire day and now her stomach was protesting. She heard the door knock. She walked up to it, her mind too blank to think.

When she opened it and saw Sam her heart stopped. She immediately thought the best and embraced Sam. But she felt his stiffness and pulled away. His face was serious, and she gave him a curious look, not sure as to why he was acting so standoffish.

CHAPTER 21

The boat engine started when it was given a second pull. It sputtered then purred to life. Sam and Justin stood around Clement, who was working the engine, hoping that they wouldn't attract any attention. Clement pulled up the anchor, and soon they were on their way.

Sam hadn't been comfortable asking Adele for this favor. It ate him up inside, made him feel like he was using her. That look she gave him when she saw him at the door melted his conscience, like he was hurting her just by being there. Her joy was sapped away when he told her why he came back. He started to explain, but she raised her hand to silence him and walked to her father's room. He heard a few words in French and what sounded like Adele pleading. Then Adele and her father came out.

Justin came up to Sam who was looking over the starboard side. "He says he knows the part of Corsica, which we're heading to, pretty well."

"Yeah?" Sam was surprised that Justin had actually engrossed Adele's father in a conversation. He was more surprised that he hadn't heard them talking. Not a good sign. The last thing he needed was to go into a mission with something on his mind. Especially one as dangerous as this one. Sam'd seen a few guys in Iraq lose focus because of problems at home. Then when they were on missions, important missions, they lost focus because they'd been thinking about their wives cheating on them. That's when it happened, an ambush, and they were caught off guard.

Sam knew his friend needed him. Whatever he had with Adele was irrelevant now.

"Yeah man," Justin looked at his friend, a curious look on his face. "Once we get out to the open seas we'll look over the maps with him."

"Cool, good deal," Sam said, trying to say something that would show he was interested in this, but his heart wasn't in it.

"You good man?" Justin patted Sam's back.

"Yeah, I'll be fine man." Sam gave a halfhearted smile. "You know how it goes sometimes."

"Right man," Justin said, nodded his head, and smiled in unison with Sam. "She's one hell of a chick, huh?"

Sam didn't react except to stare harder at the black sea. "Yeah... fuck." He shook his head.

"Don't worry man," Justin said. "This kinda stuff will work out. It always does. You two look perfect together..."

"I know man. Don't worry about me."

"I do worry about you Sam. You shouldn't hold back all the time."

"Yeah I know."

"I know, I know. Stubborn son of a bitch, aren't ya? Why do I even try?"

Sam smiled.

"I'm here Sam... I'll always be here." Justin placed his hand around Sam's shoulder.

"Thanks Justin," Sam said. "I appreciate it—really I do. But I'll be fine. Let's get this fucker."

Justin looked back and forth between Sam's eyes, "let's."

The two friends stared at the few boats they passed in silence. Just being in each other's presence, each of their minds started going over the possible scenarios that they could face in a few hours. Soon Sam had pushed even the smallest thought of Adele to the back of his mind. He had a job to do, and nothing was going to stop that now.

When they had reached a decent cruising speed, Clement beckoned them over to the wheel. He already had maps laid out and he indicated that they might want to look over them. Sam and Justin stared blankly at the maps. They could make out the coast line where they wanted to go, but realized they didn't know any more than that. Their original plan had been to come from inland. Sam looked at Justin and rolled his eyes, they were unprepared.

Clement looked over his shoulder. The lack of sound or maps rustling grabbed his attention. He slowed the boat down and turned to address them. He took a moment to size up these two men. Most of it was directed towards Sam. Here was a man whom his daughter was in love with and for whom Clement was doing this favor.

Clement wondered why his beautiful daughter had fallen for such a man. Physically he was lean, but his features were average. His scars only added to this lack of handsomeness as if to accent Sam's looks with glitches of a pen, and the tattoos only reminded Clement of so many men he'd known who tried to show their toughness by inking their skin. Clement had never been one to go for such symbolic acts. It seemed that Sam's personality was as thick as paper.

Clement could see their apprehension and decided he'd stared long enough. "So where exactly do you two want to go?" he asked.

Justin and Sam glanced at each other in uncomfortable silence. "A little north of this town," Justin said as he pointed to Bastia.

Clement glanced at where Justin's finger was pointed and nodded his head. "Okay, do you have any idea where exactly?"

"Right here," Sam pulled out the piece of paper where he'd written the description of the area and threw it on the map.

Clement glanced at it and grinned. He knew where this was. He'd been there before. What Sam wanted with the area was beyond him. "All right this should be no problem. I know where this is."

Then it hit him, as the words came out his mouth. He looked at Sam again. Now more of it was starting to make sense. Sam's scars, mannerisms, the reason why Adele came even somewhat close to considering this man. Clement whistled out loud. Clement was surprised he hadn't seen it earlier. He'd been away from the military for so long that he hadn't thought about it.

"Well, we want to get as close as possible," Sam said, looking a little confused. "Without being heard of course."

"Of course," Clement said, his mind racing. "So tell me Sam, what did you do before this?"

Sam stared at Clement. "Why do you ask?"

"I think that's obvious don't you? Just because you're taking my daughter for a ride doesn't mean you can take me for one." Clement now turned around and gently slowed the boat down until it had come to a complete stop.

"I was in the Army," replied Sam.

Clement nodded his head at Justin. "You too I'll assume?"

"Yeah," Justin said, slightly off key.

"Two ex-military men, using a boat in the middle of the night to sneak onto the shoreline. So what are you two doing right now?"

"Nothing really," Sam said.

"Oh really?" Clement could see Sam's character better in this situation. Stress always tended to bring out the true outlines of people's beings. He could see that Sam would make a stand and not back off. Stubbornness in the face of overwhelming odds. Not always a good trait—rarely a bad one. "Funny thing I heard earlier this morning, when I talked to my friend at the dock." Clement searched both their faces to see any reaction. "He said some one had tried, though they failed, to kill a local crime boss." He could see from the small nuanced change in each of their eyes that something had registered. "You guys know anything about that?"

"Naw, no clue, crime can get out of hand sometimes," said Sam.

"Oh, well I apologize then. Because for a second when you pointed out the house that you wanted me to bring the boat closer to. The house that Pyotr has probably run to for safety, since it was he that someone tried to kill last night. Well I thought that you two were behind it all." Clement paused for a reaction.

"All right," Sam raised his hands. "So what do you want to know?"

"I want to know everything."

CHAPTER 22

Adele couldn't sleep, though she tried. Her thoughts were too loud. She grabbed her purse and walked outside. It was another beautiful summer night in Nice. There was a cool breeze moving the palm trees. She walked until she got to the Promenade. There were still a few people out. Couples of all ages enjoying a stroll. Young drunken kids walked by either starting or finishing their pub-crawl through *Vieux* Nice.

The black sea was unreceptive and quiet. Refusing to communicate any clue as to what was happening beyond the horizon. Adele leaned over the wall next to the beach. She tried to will something from the darkness, but nothing would come.

That dreaded feeling in her stomach was still there, and she felt nothing could take it away. The only two men she'd ever loved were out there somewhere, and she felt like she was going to lose them.

Laughter and loud voices interrupted her thought. She looked over and saw a group of kids taking off their clothes near the beach. First one man jumped in, then a trio of girls. One last man was hesitatingly taking his clothes off. He put down his glasses ever so gently on the pebble beach and followed the rest of them into the water. There followed some screams and more laughter.

She walked back to *Vieux* Nice. The hordes of drunks thickened. Adele headed for the cafe where she knew someone. She tried opening the door, but it was closed. She peered inside and could see a shape moving about. She knocked on it, softly at first, but as the urgency of having to talk to someone increased, she knocked harder. The shape stopped its movement then walked up to the door. Adele gave a half wave as the man peered out. The door unlocked, and she walked in.

"Adele!" The man opened his arms and gave her a hug.

"Florian," Adele said and gave him a kiss on each cheek. "So great to see you."

"Ahh, so what brings you here at this time?" Florian led her up to the bar and switched on a light. "Why the long face Adele?"

Adele gave a pained smile. "A lot on my mind." Florian had been her father's friend since before she could remember and she always knew him as being someone the family had always counted on.

Adele also knew this was where she'd first spotted Sam. She glanced over at the table she had first seen him. Something calmed her down. She could almost picture Sam sitting there.

"Come on Adele." Florian's hand rested on her wrist, and he gave her a fatherly smile. "Sometimes just talking can help you know?"

"I know Florian, I know." She gave him a look, then decided she would let go a little. "I'm just worried."

"About what?" Florian waited a little more than a customary pause before raising his eyebrows. "You know there was a murder down the street last night?"

"Really?" Adele was surprised for no more than a second before she thought of Sam.

"Oh yes." Florian pointed down the street. "Right there at that restaurant."

Adele followed his eyes to where he was pointing, and she felt nauseous. Sam never did tell her what he was doing when she'd first seen him. But now as Florian pointed out where the murder had taken place, she knew. He was stalking his prey. When she thought of it like that, it sent a chill down her spine. "Oh?"

"Yes, two men apparently walked in and, without anyone seeing them, walked upstairs and tried to kill Pyotr." Florian paused. "You know who he is?"

"No."

"He's a big boss out here." Florian paused to let that sink in.

"Oh?"

"Yes. Russian Mafia."

"But he got away?"

"Yes, his body guard got shot first. So Pyotr jumped out the window and ran away."

"And no one else got hurt?"

"No one else. The police say it was probably some mafia rivalry. They say it was professionally done. Well you know what they say, 'you reap what you sow'."

"Yes, I know." Adele nodded thoughtfully at the cliché. Professionally done. That sent another chill through her spine.

"But you didn't come here to hear about murder. Tell me what's bothering you Adele."

Adele was still letting the information about Sam set in. "Well papa just left in the middle of the night to go off in his boat," she said, not really knowing why she was lying to Florian.

"Oh?"

"Yes, I'm really worried, I have no idea why," she said. "He was really secretive, do you have any idea why?"

Florian was looking down pretending to rearrange some glasses when he was actually thinking about how he should break this news to Adele. He looked up. "Do you know what your father does for a living Adele?"

"No. I know he doesn't fish anymore."

"That's right. No money in that, but he does use his boat a lot right?"

"Right," she said.

"Adele... your father is a smuggler."

Adele gave a slight smile at what appeared to be a ludicrous accusation. She had always suspected it, but never truly thought it possible. Her father was too saintly for that.

"No it's true. You see when your mother got ill the bills started to pile up very quickly because they had to send her to America for some special treatment. Your father couldn't spend all that time away. So he had to give up fishing. To pay the bills he ran into someone who paid him very well for using his boat to smuggle a few things here and there. That man was very kind to your father and helped him out when he needed it the most. You can't blame him Adele... He needed the money and your mother was sick. Such things will drive a man to do almost anything."

"I know," said Adele. "He loved mama so much."

"As he loves you, but that's why he must have left tonight. Pyotr was the man who helped him out whenever he needed it." Florian made a motion towards the restaurant where the hit had taken place. "Your father was quite fond of him and was willing to do almost anything for him. They were almost one in the same. Almost certainly Pyotr needed a favor and your father was more than willing to comply. Pyotr may be a crime boss Adele, but he is a very fair man. It was because of him that your mother lived so long."

Her head started spinning. She had to get out now. Get out and get some fresh air. Things seem to have gone from bad to worse. "Sorry Florian, I have to go," Adele stood up and walked quickly out the door.

The boat sped across the sea. Clement was at the helm. He was looking out for other boats, making certain to stay out of their way. His mind stewed in all the information Sam had thrown at him.

Sam and Justin were out here to kill Pyotr.

Clement's initial reaction had been shock. Clement knew both these men were ex-military, men who had been through combat— he respected that. But the audacity to attempt a hit on an organized crime syndicate was over the top. Yet even as Clement was silently mocking their foolhardiness, the fire in their eyes struck a chord with him. And still, the bottom line was Sam was trying to kill Pyotr, a man who was very dear to Clement.

Their reason seemed legitimate enough. No one would ever say that avenging your sister's death was overboard. Not in Clement's world, but he really didn't care about the sister. He hadn't known her. He'd heard about a couple getting killed for stealing a large amount of cocaine from Pyotr some time ago. Clement hadn't listened to the details of the story. It'd seemed like some punk kids got too big for their shoes and paid with their lives. For Clement this was all well, for such irrational characters cause instability in the world.

Clement looked over his shoulder at the sound of a moan. Justin vomited his insides over the side of the boat. Apparently this was his first time on a boat, and he was taking some time to grow his sea legs. Clement laughed out loud. Justin finally settled to take a nap. It angered Clement that they were so confident. They had no reason.

CHAPTER 23

Pyotr slammed down the phone. He'd arrived at his summer home eight hours ago. Last night, in Nice, he ran to *Le Port* where he met up with an old friend who helped sneak him out here. Now that he was here, he wasn't so sure if it was a good idea. With him were five of his most faithful men. It was all he could muster on such a short notice. This was his inner circle; he'd known them his entire life. Three of them were muscle men, not too bright, but good at what they did and willing to do anything he asked. The other two were thinkers, and they were trying to come up with a plan for the next move.

First thing had been to secure the house and the outlying areas. Pyotr's summer home was never meant to be a safe house. It was his place to get away from the tiresome work in Nice. His wife and three kids were here and the last thing he wanted was to endanger their lives. The only road in was a dirt road off the main highway. They blocked with tree logs. The sea was only a few hundred meters away, but the rocks around the coast nearby would make any sort of boat landing there foolish. Pyotr placed a man on each of the two entrances to the house. Anything else was beyond their capabilities. They would rotate, making sure they were well rested. The yard around the house wasn't well lit, but the two people outside would be able to see most movement and hear noises fairly easily. They each had a radio so they could communicate.

Pyotr knew he couldn't stay here for too long. A day at the most, then they would move on. He was glad his family, who were out here on vacation, wasn't harmed. End the bloodline: it was this most basic and primitive of acts that had scared him. His own death wasn't much of a concern, leaving nothing in this world was.

His first reaction was that Fyodor had sent out a hit on him. It was based on a gut feeling Pyotr had been having for quite some time. Fyodor was after Pyotr because of jealousy. If this was true, life was going to get very hard very quick. If Pyotr had to strike back, it wouldn't be easy. Fyodor was powerful and smart. He wasn't Pyotr's boss without reason. If he'd done this Pyotr would have to go after him until one of them was dead. To add to Pyotr's confusion Fyodor called.

"Hello Pyotr?"

"Yes?" answered Pyotr.

"This is Fyodor, are you okay?"

"Yes, yes I made it out fine," Pyotr said, wondering if this was a rouse.

"My condolences Pyotr. I heard about Aleksei."

"Yes, he's... gone." Pyotr could feel his heart race.

"He was a good soldier. One of the best."

"Yes, he was," replied Pyotr.

"Don't worry. I'll have all my men at your disposal. We will get whoever did this, you understand?"

"Yes of course."

"Do you have any clue?"

"No I don't, Fyodor."

"We'll find them, don't worry." And Fyodor hung up.

Pyotr's friends were trying to convince him to look inside their own organization for a possible suspect. Yet they couldn't come up with any names. So the consensus was that they'd have to go back to Nice. Get back there and start getting some people to talk. Do whatever they could to get a lead. But the last thing Pyotr wanted was to go back to Nice and get ambushed by Fyodor.

With the two guards posted outside, Pyotr decided to go to sleep. His forty-five handgun was in his hands, with his arms crossed across his chest. Locked and loaded. He wasn't going to get caught with his pants down this time. He made sure that his wife and kids were in one room, locked from the inside. Pyotr closed his eyes as he tried to get some rest. Good men he trusted were here to watch after him. He was safe. Tomorrow he would have to make the decision.

Clement turned off the engine. When everything went silent Sam and Justin slowly got up, trying to be as quiet as possible. Clement looked them over impatiently and made a motion with his hand so that they'd come over. Every action of theirs infuriated him.

When they came over, he told them where they were. They would pull the boat in. There wouldn't be anyone around to see them. This area was too rural. The rocks here were too dangerous for anyone but a smuggler. He pointed out how far away the house was. Less than a kilometer.

Sam and Justin looked at each other. Further than they had anticipated, but not completely out of the question. Besides this way they could be certain that their insertion wouldn't be noticed.

As they were thinking out loud Clement slowly turned and walked away from the map.

"Uh, Clement," Sam said and reached out his hand to stop him, but pulled it back. "Is there a trail or something to the house?"

Clement turned around again. "Don't worry about that Sam."

"Why not?"

"Because, Sam." Clement placed an American accent behind Sam's name. "I'm coming with you." With that Clement turned around again and walked into the cabin.

Sam and Justin exchanged a look. Justin mouthed the words 'what the fuck?'

Sam nodded his head and moved to follow Clement. It wasn't necessary; Clement came out with a rifle in his hands and a box full of bullets. He laid both on the table.

"Clement, I..." Sam glanced at Justin. "We don't think you should come with us."

"And why is that Sam?" Clement gave a smirk.

"Well..." Sam didn't like this. "It's just too dangerous of a mission for you."

"Really? You know about my past as I'm sure Adele has told you, right?"

"Yes, but that was forty years ago, right?"

"Okay, so let me ask you. Do you have any idea of what you're getting into?" Clement paused. "Let me guess, you have no idea do you? Pyotr isn't someone who you can just walk into his house and shoot. He's a mob boss so that means he's dealt with this kind of thing before. You two got lucky when you did that hit in Nice. You missed him when he was unaware and with only one other person. Now he's on the alert you think you'll fare better? What I do know about Pyotr is that he has five men he can trust completely at all times. Those men will be by his side tonight. So against five men you think you have a chance? I at least have some knowledge of how to get to him, what this house looks like from the outside, and a little from the inside. It may not be much, but it's a lot more than you two know." Clement then picked up his rifle. "And I'm still a good shot, and tonight you two are going to need all the help you can get."

On land, Sam and Justin followed Clement. They froze when Clement came to a stop. They mimicked Clement as he got down and low-crawled up to a bush. Sam and Justin crawled up to Clement. When they were all in line he pointed out the house. They were no more than fifty meters away, and though they couldn't hear anything, they could make out a figure standing in the darkness. The single-story house wasn't that big. Clement nodded at them and crawled back. After they were certain they were far enough away that they couldn't be heard they got in a huddle.

"You saw the guard right?" Clement whispered.

They nodded.

"You can be certain there's another one on the other side of the house. So that's two on the outside. I said before no less than five friends so inside there will be four other men." He looked at Sam and Justin trying to let this all sink in. "At a minimum."

"How thick are those doors?" asked Justin.

"Not too thick, you'll be able to knock them down, though maybe not you." Clement looked at Sam to give his slight. "So do you have any plan whatsoever?"

"Yeah. We have a plan," said Sam.

Pyotr awoke from his sleep. He was sweating and couldn't quite remember where he was or what he was doing on a sofa. A few seconds of looking around, and he came to his senses. His dream had felt very real. He tried to recall details. But aside from the pit feeling in his stomach, and the doubt in his head, the dream hadn't left much of a trail.

The room was dark, and Pyotr tried to make out of some of the shapes: his summer home in Corsica. With that thought came a flash of the dream. He'd been running. A dark figure chasing him. He couldn't keep it from coming after him.

This place isn't safe. That feeling hit Pyotr like a train. Did the dream itself wake him up or did something in this world do it? As he felt the quiet all around him, Pyotr suppressed his gut instinct. He was never one to do so lightly. His instinct had always been there for him. It was just that usually there was some clue that he could seize upon as evidence that his instinct was right.

His father always told him that he should listen to his dreams. That it was God's way of trying to speak to you. Pyotr never really bought that. What had listening to dreams done for his father? He died married to the bottle before Pyotr turned ten.

He looked down at his shirt. There was a patch of sweat. The forty-five in his right hand was dangerously close to slipping out from his wet hands. He wiped off the hand and held the gun in a snug comfortable grip.

Clement crawled around to the edge of a clearing south of the house. Clement lay still for a minute trying to listen for anything out of place. Seeing if the guard might have somehow heard him. Only his heartbeat broke the night's silence.

The guard looked tired and shifted his weight from one leg to the other. Clement finally took a deep breath and rolled to one side and unslung his rifle. It was a 30.06 rifle, a favorite of his. Though it had been a long time since he had a live target in its sights. He unslung it as slowly as possible. His joints groaned. It took him over a minute, and he would have taken longer if not for his shaking muscles. He was too old for this. When he had the rifle in both hands, he slowly rolled to his front.

Clement slowly brought the rifle up to his shoulder and propped it up on his elbows. Sam's plan of initiation was weak. Clement was only to fire if he heard shots.

Clement closed his eyes. He couldn't shake Adele's image out of his mind. In the last few days her face went from somber and solemn to a joyous glow. That smile that she had as a young child was finally back. When she left for Africa, it hurt Clement. She'd send a card every now and then. Clement would open them hoping for a picture of that smile. But it never came. All of those pictures were empty images of the daughter he wanted to remember.

When Clement's wife died. Life seemed to collapse all around him. That's when Adele came back. Life had a purpose again. Still Clement wanted to see that smile. His daughter had come back quieter than before, and her body seemed to be squeezed of any happiness. He forgot about the smile and just tried to get her to talk. But she was depressed, and Clement was unable to help her out. Then one day she had a glow on her face. He caught it from the corner of his eye. And Sam was the reason for the smile.

Clement opened his eyes and looked for the guard. The guard was still there, and he seemed to be nodding off. Then Clement saw another guard come out. They mumbled a few words to each other then switched out. Clement took a mental note of this and hoped that Sam was doing the same. The odds had just gotten worse. With the guards switching out it meant that the two on the outside would be more alert, as well as the two just going in.

As his finger laid to rest outside the trigger guard, Clement slowed his breathing and steadied his position as he waited for the starting pistol.

Sam and Justin came to the last bush before the clearing. The guard on the northern side was leaning up against the door and fairly quiet.

They crept up to the side of the house, crouching low. It had been almost five minutes since they'd split with Clement. There was something in Clement's eyes that told Sam the old man was up to something. Sam looked at his friend as they edged to the corner. They passed underneath a window. They also made sure not to rub the walls. Sam could feel his blood rushing everywhere. He was scared, but he knew what to do.

Justin looked back at Sam. Sam gave a smirk and a hang loose signal. Justin grinned and turned back to the corner. Sam squeezed Justin's shoulder. His friend turned the corner.

CHAPTER 24

Rasputin'd always been more of a thinking man so pulling guard was a nice change of pace. He'd been surprised that Pyotr was almost killed the night before. Who could have done it? Whoever it was, Rasputin was certain it was no inside job. They would've heard the rumblings of a plan if it had been.

Rasputin took a deep breath. It was a beautiful night. The full moon lit the landscape in an eerie glow. He always loved Corsica. It was a beautiful island, and he enjoyed spending his hard earned time-off here soaking up the sun on the beaches. Too bad they were here under these circumstances. He'd been looking forward to taking some time off—money was good. Then last night happened and changed everything.

They had to shift their resources towards hurting people and finding some answers. Rasputin never liked that, yet he knew it was a necessary evil. Rasputin thought about the last time he came to Corsica, near Ajacio, his family in tow. He remembered a cute frail Finnish girl he met. Rasputin stared wistfully at the stars in remembrance of the night with the young girl. She had claimed to be twenty, but had been painfully more innocent than that.

Rasputin may have been daydreaming, but his mind was sharp that night. When he heard the snap his brain immediately assessed it as a threat. Nothing except for a large moving animal could have made that distinct crunch. He spun his head towards the direction of the noise and he saw two shadows creeping up on him. One man walked in a crouched position. The other was behind him. Each had a handgun. The man behind had his weapon above the second man's shoulders.

Rasputin froze for a second. His mind sent a message to his mouth to say something. As the words were about to be spoken, he realized how foolish it was. He reached for his weapon. His own gun was where it should have been, tucked in the front of his pants. Locked, loaded with the safety off. He should've pulled the gun out as soon as his brain sensed something wrong. If he had he might have shot one, and though he would've been finished by the other, taking one out would have rendered the two men's mission all but impossible.

But he didn't. By the time his hand touched his weapon, all he saw was a blinding flash. He heard nothing more.

Yuri never liked standing around doing nothing, and this was especially boring. He always hated being the one picked to do the boring jobs. It had been this way when he was young. After working his way up the mafia's food chain he had been allowed other jobs. Now an emergency had arisen, he was at the bottom of the chain. Tomorrow they would be on their way back to Nice. Yuri didn't make decisions or play much of a part in them; he was good at following orders. That was all.

Yuri looked around as he thought he heard some movement out in the woods. He relaxed when he realized it was just the wind picking up. He was sure that nothing was going to happen tonight, and Pyotr was being paranoid. Justifiably so, almost getting your life taken raises your imagination slightly. Yuri was furious that Aleksei had been killed. Who ever did this would have to pay. Though Yuri wouldn't be making any plans, he would be doing the grind work. Getting names and following through with threats. Yuri thought with satisfaction of all that was ahead. He had a knack for violence and always relished a chance to excel at it. He might even increase his standings with Pyotr.

It was a few split seconds before the sound waves from the shot hit his ears. The sound scared him. His mind tried to contemplate what was going on. It came from the other side of the house. He turned to enter the house. He didn't hear the second shot. He didn't even see it. The bullet ripped through the back of his head and sprayed the door in front of him with a mixture of liquid and mist composed of his face and brain matter. His body hit the door after the bullet pushed through and crumpled into a pile of flesh.

Pyotr got up after an hour's worth of sleep. He was still tired, but something had woken him up again. The room was quiet. Pyotr was sure a guard change was what woke him up. One of the two men in his room rustled as if to indicate that Pyotr's movement was too much. Pyotr walked to the master bedroom and slowly opened the door.

His wife was sleeping, and his two children were next to her. He walked as quietly as he could and sat down next to her. She moaned a disgruntled sound. Her eyes slowly opened halfway, she looked up at Pyotr, and her frown turned into a smile. Pyotr smiled back and took her hand. Her presence helped assuage his fears.

"Is everything all right?" she asked.

"Yes." Pyotr took her hand and touched it to his cheek. He closed his eyes and felt it. Soft and with that aloe-lotion smell she always applied before she went to bed. In another life he would have written poems about it. In this one he would simply have to appreciate it. He slid her hand over to his lips, kissed her fingers, and opened his eyes. "Everything is going to be fine."

She looked at Pyotr, her face confused.

Pyotr leaned in to give her a kiss. He felt the comfort of her lips.

Pyotr jerked back. His wife did the same. The sound distinct. Each warm thought was quickly replaced with thoughts of dread. Pyotr didn't hesitate for a second. He knew exactly what was coming. He grabbed his wife's weapon and cocked it back before he handed it to her. She took it hesitatingly.

"I'm going out baby," Pyotr looked into her eyes trying to summon a response from her.

The second shot went off. Pyotr's heart raced.

The kids woke up and though they were silent Pyotr knew they had to be consoled. She would have to be confident enough to do so. "Stay in here, block the door with a chair, and shoot anyone who walks in. Okay?"

"Okay, I love you," she said. Her hand was still on his as he got up.

Two more shots went off. From the walls' vibrations one could tell it was in the house now.

"I love you too." Pyotr pulled out his handgun and opened the door. Before he left, he turned around. "Lock the door and shoot anyone who breaks in. Get under the bed and stay down!" Another two shots fired off. With the door open the sound was deafening. He turned back around and walked to his fight.

THE KILL

The party had been going on all night and Damien was getting tired of his friends. He'd tried to invite as many people as he knew, but this place was getting out of hand. There had to be at least a hundred people in the house right now; he barely recognized any of them.

From across the room he saw Kate. They caught each other's eyes. The industrial techno was playing far too loudly for them to hear each other, but from Kate's smile and follow me gesture, Damien knew what was coming next.

He walked up the stairs, grabbed a hold of her, pulled her close, and gave her a kiss. They walked up to their room. Damien pulled out his key, but it was already open. He was annoyed that some one would have opened it, as no one else should have the key, but he forgot about it as he grabbed Kate and threw her on the bed. He tore off his shirt and took a step towards her. Her look of anticipation was replaced with one of curiosity. She wasn't looking at him either. She was looking behind him.

"What's wrong baby?" As soon as Damien finished the sentence, his neck whipped back as a kick caught him in the lower back. He went flying into Kate and couldn't help but land an elbow on her chest.

"Hello Damien," Pyotr said.

All the color was sucked out of Damien's face. "Hello Pyotr."

Kate recoiled in horror.

"Is this the famous Kate?" Pyotr asked.

"Kate?" Damien gave his best inquisitive look.

Pyotr's face darkened. He grabbed Damien and threw him against the wall. When Kate stood up, Pyotr stepped up to her and gave an open palm upper cut to her nose. The cracking sound of her nose breaking filled the room. She fell back on the bed, her nose started to bleed.

"Kate!" Damien tried to reach for her, but two men grabbed him. One took out some rope and tied his hands behind his back. Then his feet were bound together.

Aleksei leaned him up against the wall. "Don't worry, all right?" He gave a smile then landed a crushing blow into Damien's stomach. Damien doubled over and, still trying to suck for air, fell to the ground.

"You assholes! Damien!" Kate yelled out. The two men came over and held her down. When they stepped back they'd tied her, each limb to a bedpost.

"So you little shits thought you were going to fuck me over and just waltz out of town?" Pyotr said calmly.

Neither of them said a word.

He looked over at Kate. "Was it your idea, honey?"

"No! It was me," Damien blurted out.

"I don't think so, Damien." Pyotr sat down next to Kate. "It was this bitch who made you do it. Right, honey?"

"Fuck you," Kate spat out.

"No sweetheart." Pyotr smirked. "I do believe it's fuck you." He got up and nodded at his two men. One walked over to Damien, grabbed him by the hair, and jerked his face so that he could see Kate and nothing else. The other walked over to Kate and pulled out his knife.

"No please Pyotr, don't," pleaded Damien.

"Too late for that now isn't Damien?" Pyotr said and turned away.

Kate clenched her teeth as Aleksei put out a cigarette on her belly. She squirmed when she saw him put a lighter to the knife. Aleksei gave her a dirty smile.

"Just tell me where the money is and this will be over as soon as possible," Pyotr said.

"I..." Damien trailed off because he didn't know where the money was. He had told Kate to go and hide it before the party. She had kept it a secret from him. She always did that. But now all hope was lost for saving her life. The beat of the techno downstairs shook the room.

Pyotr gave a nod to Aleksei then turned away. After a few seconds Kate began to scream. Pyotr looked at Damien. "Just tell me Damien and it will be over."

Damien started to cry. "I don't know." He looked up at Kate. It was over. He knew it. "Baby, I love you."

Kate screamed. The hot knife took out her nipples and now moved to her groin area.

"Aleksei, stop." Pyotr took out his gun. "Kate, look at me," he said as he walked in front of Damien and waited until he had Kate's full attention. He pointed the gun at Damien's head and pulled the trigger. Damien fell over and started twitching.

"Damien! No!" Kate screamed and almost seemed like she would break free of her bonds. She slumped back down after a few seconds. Her eyes welled up, and she started to cry.

Pyotr sat down next to her. "Tell me where it is Kate."

Kate murmured something back at Pyotr.

Pyotr picked up his phone and called someone. After speaking on the phone for a minute Pyotr hung up. "Good girl." His finger caressed her chin. His other hand was behind her with his gun. He jerked her face forward and pulled the trigger. Her face sprayed over the bed and wall. Pyotr got up. He nodded to Aleksei who carved a word on her belly. Pyotr walked out the room and into the hallway. The bass from the music hit him as he walked down the stairs. The music was so loud he could barely hear himself think. None of the kids paid attention to him and his two cohorts as they walked out.

CHAPTER 26

Justin and Sam turned the corner. Sam behind Justin, with Justin crouched to maximize their firepower. Two steps after turning the corner Justin stepped on a twig. The man standing guard at the door, five feet away, turned. Justin stopped. He kept his eye on the front sight post, and squeezed the trigger. He could see the man's head jerk back as it embraced the bullet. Justin leapt forward.

Time was now of the essence. The first shot had been fired, and everyone in the house had been alerted. Any extra time and the people inside would erect a proper defensive posture.

Justin stepped over the guard. Sam reached down and pulled out the weapon from the man's pants. As Sam tucked in the extra weapon, another shot rang out. It was a rifle. Clement had moved his piece.

Justin tested the doorknob. His eyes met Sam's. He nodded and kicked the door. The door flew open. Justin stepped inside with his weapon raised. Sam followed right behind. They moved into the darkness of the house looking for the next challenger.

Clement erased his mind of all the cumbersome thoughts when he heard the shot go off. He held his breath, kept the sights on the guard's head, and slowly squeezed the trigger. Clement felt the rifle's powerful kick as he followed through with his squeeze. The guard crumpled up in front of the back door. Clement looked at the body, dazed. He squeezed his eyes shut.

A door was kicked in. Those two were better than he'd thought. A shot and a door getting kicked in within a matter of seconds. The men inside would be scared out of their minds, and though they would fight back, they wouldn't know how many men were coming after them. Right now Justin and Sam held the advantage.

Clement lay for a second thinking. Sam had told him to stay here and shoot anyone who tried to escape through the back door. It was probably the dumbest thing Clement heard from the young man's mouth. In this darkness how was anyone supposed to discern the dark shapes coming from the house? It was a recipe for disaster. After a few seconds, Clement rose to his feet.

Sam and Justin walked into a long hallway with three doors to the left, a sitting room to the right, and a living room at the end.

Justin faced down the hallway as Sam looked in the sitting room. He saw a shadow move. He fired twice. He knew he hit it from the way the shadow twitched away. But it didn't fall. Instead it yelled. Sam walked towards the shadow. He switched on his flashlight and highlighted the chubby man with a bloodied stomach. His face was ready to take Sam on. The chubby man held a shiny handgun that was fast being raised towards Sam.

Sam squeezed off two more rounds. One round hit the man in his chest, reeling him backwards. Another hit him in his neck. Not pretty, but the man dropped. Sam switched off the flashlight. He grabbed the weapon from the man's loose grip and listened for a second as the man gargled on his own blood.

Sam and Justin were in the hallway when two shots went off. They shot back. Sam dove right to the kitchen, and Justin dove through the last door on the left.

Justin turned as soon as he dove into the room. On the floor, he looked for movement of any sort. It was empty. Justin got up on one knee. A barrage of fire exploded through the house. He hit the ground as a few shots whistled by him. He fired back through the wall.

"Fuck, Justin!" Sam yelled out. He was in the kitchen, which was separated from the living room by a counter. He hugged the ground. The refrigerator hissed as bullets ripped it. He held his head down as glass and debris rained on his body. He fired a few shots back without looking.

Justine knew they were outgunned and rushing would do no good. He looked at the window and an idea hit him. "Hey Sam!" he said and pointed towards the window.

"Okay!" Sam yelled back, and watched Justin disappear through the window. Sam waited a second. Bullets were still flying overhead. Justin would need some support and if Sam didn't provide it then this flanking movement would be over before it began. Sam changed magazines on his nine millimeter and tucked it into the front of his pants. Then he grabbed the two other weapons he'd collected, making sure each was locked and loaded, and steeled himself for what he was about to do next. His throat was tight, and he wondered if this was the moment he died.

The lull came. He heard the men shout something to each other. It could've been a ploy to draw a peek out of him, and a chance for them to shoot him in the face. But he had to take that risk. Sam took a deep breath and stood up. He started firing his two guns.

Sam kept shooting and aimed at two things: to the left, a long couch; to the right, a table lying on its side.

Sam ducked as someone from behind the table fired off two shots. From behind the couch another two shots fired. Sam knew that they were firing without looking. The table was too thick to penetrate. He kept one handgun trained above the table, and with his other handgun pointed the other gun at the couch, he fired two shots. To complement it, he fired to make certain whoever was behind the table knew they were still being tracked.

Then he heard the window, on the left side of the enemy's room shatter as a chair came flying through, followed by a figure.

143

Justin. Sam fired off all his remaining bullets. He pulled out his final handgun and spun into the hallway, keeping an eye on the table.

With a chair as a shield in one hand, and his gun in the other, Justin did a short sprint to bay window. Throwing the chair, he smashed the window, and as he jumped through a shard of glass tore through his right forearm.

Then he heard the shots coming at him. Justin could feel them hit his left side. It felt warm. He fired into the dark shadow that was right in front of him next to a coach. Justin turned on his flashlight. His three shots hit the chest of the man and he stumbled back as his weapon fell out of his hands. Justin saw a form leap up and disappear over another couch beside a thick table. He fired a shot and felt his nine-millimeter lock to the rear. "Black!"

Dropping to his knees, Justin reached for his magazine, fumbling in the dark. He heard Sam fire a few shots. With a new magazine in, Justin yelled, "up!"

When the sound of the rifle pierced Justin's eardrums, he knew Clement had joined the fray. Justin walked up to the couch, clenched his jaw, and waited for a lull. It was his signal to go. Justin leapt up on the couch and unloaded his weapon. His light on, he could see everything, but it was still happening faster than he could think. He blasted one man thrice in the chest. As he turned to the second man, a flash went off. Justin reeled back as a bullet tore through his chest. It threw his remaining shots off —all three missed. The man leapt over the couch and smashed through the patio glass door, tripping over Yuri's body. Justin tried to spin and get a proper shot off, but he was still reeling from being shot. A hot sensation spread through his chest. He didn't want to believe he was shot.

Shots were fired, though Justin wasn't certain who. Gaining some energy, Justin ran after the man who had tried to escape, the man who shot him. Out in the moonlight, Justin could see that the man was dead. He turned back to the house. Sam stood in front of a wounded man, pointing a rifle at him. In the kitchen Clement was observing the carnage.

Justin grabbed the rifle from Sam, and kept it pointed at the man.

"You Pyotr?" Justin asked.

Pyotr looked up, dazed. "Who are you?"

"Do you remember my sister Kate?" Justin asked. He looked into Pyotr's eyes trying to see if there was any recognition.

"Kate?"

"Yes, Kate, Damien's girlfriend."

"Her?! She sto—"

Justin fired three times into Pyotr's chest before unloading into his face. Pyotr's body slumped over. Justin grabbed Pyotr's ear and looked him at what remained of his face for any signs of life. "She was my sister." He pressed his fingers deeply into Pyotr's jugular. Justin got up. "He's dead."

Sam nodded to Justin, then heard the bedroom door knob twist. Before the door opened Sam ran at it and kicked it down. He heard a yelp. On the floor was a woman on the ground staring up at him with a mix of fear and determination. Sam heard something else and saw two kids under the bed staring at him. The woman got up and Sam saw a shiny weapon in her hand. He took one step and yanked the gun out of her hand. She seemed surprised. It was obvious she was no friend of violence. He pushed her down to the floor with all his force. She was small, and she should not have been a part of this. But he knew that he had to get the message across that she shouldn't try anything stupid. He pointed his rifle at her and saw her freeze up. The two children started crying. Sam put his finger to his lips, backed out of the room and closed the door.

Clement appeared by his side. "Let's go," he whispered. "We can't risk staying here much longer."

"Okay let's roll," Sam said. They'd spent less than a minute in the house so far, but they had to get out. Sam took one more sweep of the house, ensuring they picked up all the shells. When he felt good, they took off.

They ran as fast as they could. Justin was leaning on Sam and appeared to be doing fine with his wounds, but as they got closer to the boat Sam could feel Justin getting heavier.

They got on the boat and slid off to sea. Sam took Justin down into the boat and shined a light in his face. It didn't look good.

"You did good man, I can't fucking believe we did it," Justin said, breathing hard. "You were right."

Sam couldn't believe it either, but he was certain that he didn't deserve credit for some cocky statement he'd said a long time ago. "Naw man. You did most everything."

"Yea..." Justin's breathing grew shallower.

"Justin you good?" Sam could sense life leaving his friend, but he didn't want to believe it.

"You remember that time I talked about how I don't care what happens when I die?"

"You're not gonna die."

"Listen to me, Sam, I don't care. Just bury me out in the sea."

"Listen to *me*, Justin, you're going to fucking live."

"Shut the fuck up Sam!" Justin spat out before taking another shallow breath. His face was white as a ghost. "Promise me you'll bury me at sea."

Sam's eyes started to well up. "Yeah man, of course." Sam held Justin's head to his forehead, smelled the blood-sweat mixture, and tried to summon his friend away from death.

"Don't... forget me Sam."

Tears rolled down Sam's cheek. "I'll never forget you Justin. You're my brother."

"We are... brothers, aren't we?" Justin coughed. "And take care of Adele. You can trust her, she's good people."

"Yeah..." Sam wanted Justin to be silent, to save his energy to fight off death.

"Justin?" Sam said and pulled away from Justin and could see his eyes losing that ferocity they always had.

"Justin!?" Sam's tears streamed down his cheek and landed on Justin's unmoving chest. "Fuck, Justin. Not now man. Don't fucking leave me." Sam hugged his friend as tight as he could.

But Justin didn't reply. He was dead quiet.

CHAPTER 27

Sam took in the dark foreboding sea. He'd always thought the sea was comforting. Now it was another faceless evil. One which had swallowed his friend without much more than an air bubble in reply. The hole ripped that through his heart was gaping wide and had spread through his mind and body. The physical pain from the mission was all gone and that's what made it worse. Sam wanted to hurt himself, cut into some skin, flesh, so he could see a symbol for his pain, real pain to his suffering. He heard Clement shuffle up from the cabin and stand beside him.

Clement handed him a cigarette, and they both smoked in silence. After it was done, Clement handed Sam another one.

"I'm sorry about your friend."

Sam didn't answer.

"The good ones are always the first to go." Clement sucked in on his cigarette. "Your friend, he had a good heart, good energy... he cared about you a lot."

Sam, still silent, turned his head.

"When we were talking on the boat, we saw you standing alone... and he said to me, 'he likes your daughter, a lot Clement. You should know that. I know most dads are gonna hate the guy fucking their daughter, that's just natural. Sam... he's a strange motherfucker, but he's a good guy, with a good heart.'"

Sam shook his head and smiled. "He said that?"

Clement chuckled. "Not one to waste words on niceties, was he?"

"Did he say anything else?" asked Sam.

"No, then he walked over to you."

Clement handed Sam another cigarette and continued. "When I came back from Algeria I was frustrated and angry at... I don't know what, but there was this uncontrollable anger inside of me. At everyone, every last person who didn't go through what I did... and could have cared less about what I had to say." Clement paused to inhale a hit of nicotine. "I dedicated a lot of my energies to going against the government with the OAS. Then crime after that. It wasn't right, but it felt right. I was young and wouldn't listen to anyone. I had to find meaning somewhere else before I ended those ways."

"And what was that?"

"Marie... Adele's mother."

Sam thought about what Clement said. "I don't know what I've been chasing, or running from all this time. When something hurt I just wanted it to hurt more, just to show myself I could take it. That I was invincible... Maybe I was scared, and have been scared this entire time thinking I was being tough... I don't know. But I do know one thing. I don't want this to continue, this fucking violence. I never want to lose another friend to this shit." Sam took a long drag from his cigarette.

"Of course," Clement said. "So you done with this lifestyle, these demons?"

"Yes," replied Sam. "I am."

"Then let's bury them." Clement walked over to his rifle and threw it overboard along with all his bullets.
Sam threw overboard all the weapons they used that night. The shells he'd collected, their bullets. Everything.

About the Author:

A prolific writer who has written some of this century's most engrossing books, Grunn has always striven to write page-turners for the everyday man or woman. As a child he spent his time in class writing then, when he became an adult, turned this passion into his life. His books are sold throughout the world, and enjoyed by people of all backgrounds.

Connect with me online (and tell me what you think):

https://www.smashwords.com/
profile/view/aarongrunn

http://aarongrunn.blogspot.com/